FROM OUT OF THE LONELINESS

THE ADVENTURES OF DALTON LAIRD

A NOVEL BY
RUSSELL M. CHACE

TUKONA BOOKS LLC
P.O. Box 447; Cañon City. CO 81215

Trade Paperback ISBN: 978-1-733037-10-5

e-Book ISBN: 978-1-733037-11-2

Library of Congress Control Number: 2019905630

Printed in the United States.

10 9 8 7 6 5 4 3 2

Takona Books, LLC
Colorado

FOREWORD

ussell M. Chace has lived what he writes about, having run a trapline in Alaska by dog team.

This story represents one of the greatest tales ever told about the Alaskan Frontier. Chace is a master storyteller who has the greatest taste in heroes. He's a favorite with readers because he knows Alaska.

This book will keep you hooked on the edge of your seat and glued to your Kindle.

When I think about the great storytellers of the past, I add Russell M. Chace to that list because his feel for the Alaskan Frontier is second to none.

Paul L. Thompson—Bestselling author of
The U.S. Marshal, Shorty Thompson Series.

PROLOGUE

A light skiff of snow deadened his footsteps as the old sourdough worked his way through the willows toward the gravel bar on the subarctic river. The smell of death from the rotting carcasses of spawned out salmon, mingled with the musky scent of high-bush cranberries and wet earth, hung in the still evening air.

He was meat hunting—looking for moose, or caribou. But mostly moose. He most assuredly was not looking for what he found.

Stepping out of the willows onto the lower end of the gravel bar, he turned left and continued a few paces until he could see the upper end as well. A large grizzly fed on dead salmon that had floated up on shore. The old sourdough watched as the great bear stood on part of the fish and tore chunks of rotting flesh and entrails away with his teeth. The bear chewed twice, swallowed, and looked around, always alert for danger or competition.

The beast fascinated him, but he pushed his luck and stayed too long. The bear caught his scent and turned to face him.

Realizing his mistake, the old sourdough took a step backward and turned, but stopped and watched as the grizzly ambled closer. Turning around, he took three more steps and looked back just in time to see the grizzly break into a run. Panic-stricken, the old sourdough ran back through the willows looking for someplace, any place, to make his stand. He could hear the bear right behind him — plowing through the willows, popping his jaws, and grunting.

Time slowed to a crawl, as it does for most men in desperate situations, and he felt detached from his body, as if he were watching a picture show of himself with the beast in pursuit. He was able to think with a clarity the good Lord has provided for moments of flight or fight. As he thought, so his body did.

Just as the bear reached him, the old sourdough jumped to the side, which seemed to take forever. As the slow motion of the bear going past him played out, he heard a loud voice yell "NOOOO!" and watched himself smack the yellow pig eye of the bear with his gun butt. Still, in slow motion, the bear stumbled and his momentum carried his quarter ton of claw and fang a few feet past the old sourdough.

Shouldering his weapon, he waited for the bear to turn. Just as the bear came broadside, the old sourdough squeezed the trigger and felt it disengage, felt the recoil of the rifle, and watched the bullet leave the barrel. Fascinated, his eyes followed its vapor trail to the great beast's shoulder.

The bear's body shuddered as it absorbed the kinetic energy. The bear completed his turn and came at the old sourdough again. He tried to work the action. It wouldn't budge. Looking down at his rifle, he realized to his horror that it was jammed.

The old sourdough looked back up in time to see nothing but teeth and tongue and slobbers blocking his vision. He was on his back now, on the ground, and when or how he got there, he did not know. He smelled the feted fish breath of the bear. He heard crunching and ripping noises in his head.

Thinking he was going to die, he surrendered his fate to God's hand. Funny thing was, he was at peace... there was no pain.

CHAPTER 1

Dalton Laird and his lead dog, Bandit hiked along the base of the ridge through the forest. The footing was better than in the snow-covered muskeg tundra closer to the river. As they made their way upriver, the evening light faded and cast the spruce and birch trees into ominous shadows that eerily moved about with the movement of the northern lights dancing overhead. An occasional breeze moaned through the swaying spruce boughs and waved the naked birch limbs like bony fingers. The moon was three days past the first quarter.

They had hiked about fifteen miles as the raven flies from the mouth of the Salcha, and had only four more to go before they reached the lower cabin on Ninetyeight Creek.

Bandit stopped. Her low, throaty wolf growl, born of her wild ancestors, caught his attention. Dalton stopped and looked back at her. His eyes followed her intense gaze down onto an ox-bow bend in the river, directly upwind and to their right. Obviously, Bandit had smelled or heard something, or both.

Years of experience in the bush taught him to trust her instincts. Her instincts had saved his life and those of his other dogs several times. He wondered if an old bear was still out scrounging food for the winter, or perhaps a pack of wolves hunted along the river. Either way, it could be a problem. Dalton eased the lever of his 30-30 down to make sure the chamber held a round, then replaced the lever and cocked the hammer.

Kneeling down beside Bandit, he whispered, "What is it, girl?"

Bandit licked his face and whined. Then he heard it. The breeze carried an eerie moan from somewhere down on the riverbank and up through the forest canopy. Bandit turned her attention back toward the river, lowered her ears, and another low growl escaped her throat.

It almost sounds human, he thought.

Another moan wafted up from the shadows, accompanied by an unmistakable call for help.

"Humph... Some *Cheechako's* got himself in a fix. What's he doin' in my neck of the woods anyway?" he said aloud. Dalton thought a bit, then, looking at Bandit said, "Well, let's go see what he's got himself into. I've got a feeling this is going to change everything."

Dalton removed his pack board and stashed it under a spruce tree. Bandit took the lead and together they made their way downhill, across the spongy muskeg flats, down the riverbank, and into the willows on a gravel bar.

Without warning, Bandit stopped. The fur around her neck and down her spine stood on end as another growl rumbled from deep inside her muscular chest.

Dalton shouldered his rifle—not quite sure of what to expect. Her behavior raised his suspicions, and he knew it wasn't good. Together, they eased forward and came into a small clearing in the willow thicket. There, in the middle of the clearing, next to a driftwood log and bathed in the glow of moonlight and northern lights, lay the shivering bloody form of a man lying on a bed of crimson snow. The mingled scents of grizzly bear and blood lay thick in the cold night air.

The form moved and groaned. Dalton surveyed the area looking for the bear. If it was still alive or wounded, it might have bedded down somewhere nearby, guarding its kill. It didn't appear the bear tried to cover the wounded man with sticks and dirt, as bears often do with a kill. More than likely the bear was gone. Not wanting to take chances, Dalton knew he had to get the man away from the area.

Dalton knelt beside the bloody heap of

flesh and touched his shoulder. The man jerked, and a bearded face with wild eyes stared back at Dalton.

"It's okay, Fella. I gotcha."

"Who...who's there?" The man's voice was raspy. His teeth chattered in the cold.

Dalton ignored the question. He eased his rifle's hammer down and rested the firearm against a log, then quickly checked the man over looking for spurting blood, indicating bleeding from an artery. He could see in the dim light that this guy was pretty torn up. About eight inches of scalp with long, blood-matted hair, had torn loose in a crescent from his left eyebrow to the middle of his head. The left eye was swollen shut and blood covered his face. He looked like an older man, Dalton decided, probably in his sixties.

"Who's there?" the man repeated.

"Name's Dalton Laird. What's yours?" Dalton removed his coat.

"Jack...," the raspy voice answered. Clearing his throat, he tried again. "Jack Farley. People call me Yukon Jack."

Dalton took off his shirt, put his coat back on, and ripped his shirt into strips to use as bandages. Dalton wanted to keep Jack talking so he asked the next question that came to mind.

"How do you feel?"

"Like bear poop. I've just been et by a bear. What'd ya expect?"

Dalton gave him a half-crooked smile. "Yeah, I guess that was kind of a dumb question. What I meant to say was, where do you hurt? Can you move your legs?"

"Hell, I hurt all over. Don't know about my legs. I just came to a little while ago. I was gonna just give up and go to sleep and never wake up again, but something inside me said to holler for help one more time. So, I did."

Then he moved his legs a little and said, "Yeah, I can move 'em. But the inside of my right thigh burns like fire."

Dalton knew there was a major artery in that area, so he quickly checked but thankfully found no spurting blood. Turning back to face Jack he said, "I'm going to start bandaging you up now. I know you can't see much but you're going to be okay. Your scalp is torn loose. I'm going to start there. Then, I'll work on your leg. You've lost a lot of blood from the look of things."

A faint smile crossed Jack's face. "Well, it ain't all mine. I can tell you that. I put up a good fight, if I do say so my own self."

Dalton pushed Yukon Jack's scalp back into place and tied a bandage from under Jack's chin to the top of his head to hold it there. Then, turning his attention back to Jack's leg, he saw that his pant leg was ripped and caked with blood. Dalton could see two sets of bite marks where the teeth had punctured the flesh.

"He bit you a couple of times there. Looks like he missed the artery though. Good thing or you would've been dead in a few minutes. You're going to have a pretty good bruise. Probably some infection setting in as well." Dalton carefully wrapped the wound.

"Ain't nothin' important missing in that general area, is there?"

Dalton gave Jack a sideways look. "No, no I don't think there is. And I'm not going to check." Dalton finished wrapping the wound then stood, turned directly to him and said, "Listen, I need to get you and us out of here and up in the timber. Think you can make it?"

"I'll try. I feel so dog-gone weak though."

"Well, you're going to have to make it. I don't want to take a chance of that griz coming back and finding both of us. I'll help you, even If I have to carry you."

Yukon Jack looked up at Dalton. "I believe you could at that. You're a big man. Besides, I don't think there's much chance of that griz coming back. When he had me pinned down, I knifed him a couple of good ones in the throat. I think I got his jugular. Anyway, I'm sure I heard his death moan in the brush over yonder somewhere."

"Let's hope so. But just to be on the safe side, I got to get you out of here. Let me help you up."

Dalton stood, picked up his rifle, took a step toward Jack's head and shoulders. He, reached down with his free hand, grabbed Jack by the collar, and lifted him to his feet. Jack stood for a moment then almost fell. Dalton caught him in time.

"Wheeu... I'm kinda dizzy I guess."

"Here, put your arm around my neck and lean on me." Dalton took Jack's arm and placed it across his shoulders. "It's going to be tough going up to the timber. Come, Bandit."

Bandit moved from the shadows.

"Dadgum, that's a fine-looking husky, mister!"

"Hum?" Dalton looked at Jack. "Oh, yeah. Just don't do something foolish around her or you'll wish you was back with that grizzly."

Bandit took the lead as they slowly made their way through the willows to the river-bank. Crossing the muskeg, they had to stop every ten yards or so to let Jack rest. At one of these rest stops, Jack complained about his right side hurting and that the pain would almost take his breath away.

"Sounds like a cracked rib. It's not too much farther to the trees. I have a pack stashed under a spruce with a medical kit. When we get there, I'll build a fire and check you over real good."

It took about forty-five minutes to get back to Dalton's pack board. By then, the clouds had moved in and shrouded the moon. White flakes fell in the quiet night, coating the ground with a fresh layer of snow.

Dalton unpacked his caribou-hide sleeping bag and unrolled it under the spruce bough canopy. The ground was relatively level there and dry. He helped Jack lay down on the bag then quickly got a fire started with birch bark and squaw wood; the dead dry limbs still attached to the tree under the overhanging canopy.

There weren't many rocks away from the river, but Dalton found a few and arranged them around the fire to warm up. He dug his teakettle out of the pack, packed it full of snow and hung it over the fire. Then came the careful examination of Jack.

"I found out why your side hurts so much. It looks like he clawed you trying to turn you over or something. You got a couple of hunks of skin and muscle hanging loose."

Dalton used the boiling water to carefully bath and clean out as much debris as he could. Digging through his pack, he found a bottle of iodine and the small bag of salt he always carried and dabbed these into the open wounds under Jack's right arm. Next, he got out some thread and a needle from his sewing kit and soaked the thread in what was left of the iodine.

"You're a pretty tough old codger. When I first found you I kind of had you figured for a *Cheechako*." Dalton began to sew Jack's wounds closed.

"Well, I sure as heck feel like one now. I'm dizzy and cold. I think I'm going to pass out."

"Try to hold on 'til I get your side sewed up, then we'll get ya inside my sleeping bag. And try to hold still. My fingers are getting stiff from the cold. It must be twenty degrees or colder right now."

A few more stitches finished the job. With a lot of grunting and groaning on Jack's part, Dalton helped Jack crawl into the bag. Dalton added more wood to the fire and put a fresh pot of snow on the fire. He squatted by the fire and warmed his hands for a few minutes.

The Deputy Sheriff's training from years back bubbled to his brain and his mind searched for answers.

Who is this guy? Where did he come from and why is he here? Where is his gun? Nobody wanders in the bush without a gun. Dalton shook his head. *Oh, well. Time for that later. Right now, all that matters is saving his life.*

Dalton looked over at Jack. He had passed out, evidently from the loss of blood, pain, and shock. Jack shivered in his sleep. Dalton fished out some of the warmer rocks from the edge of the fire and packed those inside the bag around Jack to warm him up. A few minutes later, Jack stopped shivering and began to rest peacefully. Dalton figured this was a good time to work on Jack's torn scalp.

Dalton added more wood to the fire for light and warmth, and then unwrapped the bandages he had put on earlier. Dalton meticulously washed and picked out all the dirt, sticks, and gravel, then dabbed what was left of the iodine and some salt into the wound. Jack, still asleep, flinched and mumbled something unintelligible. Dalton pushed the scalp back in place and sewed it together. Jack was so far under, Dalton surmised Jack probably didn't feel a thing.

Dalton washed up. He put the supplies back in his pack, piled more wood on the fire, and plopped down against a tree trunk. He dug through his pants' pocket and pulled out a can of Copenhagen. He took a pinch and sighed deeply. He hadn't rested in over three hours. Bandit moved up next to him and lay down as close as she could get to her master. Together, they watched the intruder as he rested under the caribou-hide sleeping bag. Before long, Dalton's eyes grew heavy.

* * *

Dalton awoke, instantly aware of Jack's groaning and mumbling. Dalton moved toward Jack but stopped. He realized Jack was more than likely having a nightmare about the mauling... or something. Dalton leaned back against the tree. That 'something' bothered Dalton. He had a feeling there was more to Jack's story than met the eye.

Noticing the fire had died down, Dalton put an armload of wood on the embers. He replaced the rocks in the sleeping bag with fresh, warm ones.

Squatting next to Jack, Dalton watched Jack's chest rise and fall for a few moments. It seemed normal enough.

It's a good thing it dropped to twenty degrees or so and snowed last night, Dalton thought. *Else he probably would've bled to death. I'm surprised he didn't die from the cold. He must be a tough old bird.*

Dalton noticed it was getting light in the southeast. The snow had ceased falling. He looked at his pocket watch. It read seven twenty-five.

"Bandit, stay." He patted her on her head. "It'll be light soon and I'm going down to the river to look things over. You keep an eye on him, ya hear?"

Bandit, of course, heard but didn't understand. All she understood was her name and the word, 'stay.' She knew what that meant. She couldn't follow him. She showed her disappointment by giving him a disgusted look, turned her back to him, and settled down by the fire.

Dalton chuckled a bit. "It's okay, girl. I'll be back soon."

Bandit lay down her head and heaved a deep sigh. Dalton shook his head. "Just like a woman." He left her sulking next to the sleeping form of their new acquaintance.

CHAPTER 2

It was late in the evening when Corrine Batiste heard the voices of her father and the recently hired trappers coming from the bar area of the Amanita Saloon.

She stoked the cast iron cook stove with wood and placed the Dutch oven full of moose stew she'd made earlier on top to reheat.

"Trappers," she said, half under her breath. "Woodsmen maybe. But not trappers." She bet not one of them ever put in the hard day's work trapping requires.

"They're *dinjii naįį iizuų,*" bad people, she said, in her mother's Gwich'in Athabaskan tongue. Ward was the worst. He always seemed to be leering at her.

Tasting the moose stew, she decided it needed a little more salt. As she reached for the container on the shelf, she heard, "Mm… Mm…Mm. Sure looks good."

Corrine turned with a start toward the door

and saw Frank Ward leaning against the door post, arms folded, grinning at her.

He looks like a weasel. "What do you want?"

"You know what I want," he said, still grinning. "What the Boss wants is food on the table...for all of us."

"Tell him it's on its way. I have to make some fresh biscuits because you guys are so late," she said with obvious irritation.

"Yeah, well, we ran into a little difficulty. But we're here now." Frank's eyes took their time traveling down her body and back up. His smile drew a chill through her spine. She watched as he turned and left the kitchen.

Corrine gathered up the silverware and dishes they would need and carried them through the kitchen door. As she placed them around the table where the men sat, she eavesdropped on their conversation.

"Well, I think we ought to head back out and get as much fur as we can," the one they called Hank said.

Corrine saw her father shake his head. "*Non*! I've been checking some furs coming into Northern Commercial. They're not prime yet. I want to give 'em another week."

"Quantity over quality." Corrine glanced in the direction of the voice. It was the Swede. "From what we found, the Salcha is chock-full of fur. We stand to make a killin' right there. I say get in, get 'em, and get out."

Corrine glanced at her father as she continued setting the dishes and silverware. She watched a frown cross his face.

"Like I said, we'll give 'em a week. Then we'll have both quantity *and* quality to maximize our profits. No?"

Looking around the table, she noticed Yukon Jack was missing.

"Where's Jack?" she asked timidly.

Suddenly, everyone's attention was on her and silence filled the room. A few of the trappers glanced at each other, and then averted their eyes.

Her father, Jon Batiste said, "None of your business, *petite fille*. Go back to the kitchen and bring us some coffee. And then you can start on those biscuits."

Her skin flashed red-hot as her blood pressure rose. It always irritated her when her father called her a little girl. He had called her that from her childhood, growing up in Fort Yukon. However, she was a grown woman now. Twenty winters. And the way he said it seemed to convey a sense of superiority over her like she could never measure up.

Like the sense of superiority she felt from most of the white women and many of the Indians as well, just because she was a half-breed.

She vaguely remembered him treating her Athabaskan mother like that, those many years ago. Back before her mother had mysteriously drowned in the Yukon River when Corrine was ten winters old. The responsibility fell on Corrine to take over her mother's duties then, cleaning house, cooking, mending, laundry. She didn't know how her mother had managed.

Corrine had to grow up fast in those days. Now, she had more mouths to feed. Within the past three weeks, her father had gathered a bunch of lowlifes around him, both white and Indian. Men of questionable honor, she did not feel safe.

Yukon Jack was different. He was older. Although she had known him only a few weeks, he was always kind to her. He was a *vaanoodlit*, a white man, but she liked him and trusted him. She sensed in him an honorable man and looked on him as a grandfather. Everybody knew it, even her father. She knew he did not approve of it, and it showed in the way he treated Jack. However, she liked him and he made her laugh, unlike her father— sitting here with a smug look on his face, always calling her a little girl.

I'm taller than he is. She leaned in toward his ear. "Stop calling me little girl... little Napoleon."

Two or three snorts and snickers erupted from the men around the table as Jon Batiste's face turned red and a vein in his neck pulsated. Corrine knew she'd crossed the line. She turned and walked back into the kitchen with as much grace and dignity as she could muster, preparing for the sting of wrath to come.

The kitchen bat-wing doors slammed open and Corrine turned with a start. Jon Batiste, all five feet, five inches of him stood in the doorway glaring at her, breathing heavily. Corrine briefly imagined little puffs of steam coming from his nostrils. She almost cracked a smile. However, she didn't. She had seen and felt his anger before.

Her father walked up to her and landed a slap on her cheek that made a loud *SMACK*. Corrine's head violently jerked to her right from the impact. She raised a hand to her stinging cheek as tears welled up in her eyes, and slowly turned to face him, not saying a word.

Jon glared at her for a moment then growled, "Don't you ever do that again in front of my men, *petite fille*. By heaven, I will take a strap to you, I will. You're getting more headstrong like your mother every day, and I don't like it. And if you don't change your attitude, no man will want you and you may end up just like her. Now, I'm doing the best I can to provide for the both of us and I don't need your insolence undermining my authority in front of my men."

"Where is Jack? Did something happen to him?" Her own voice sounded weak to her ears.

"Watch yourself, *mon petite fille*. That is none of your business. Let's just say he doesn't work for me anymore and he's not coming back. Now, I'll take the coffee out and you start on those biscuits."

Jon Batiste turned, picked up a potholder then the pot of coffee, and walked out of the kitchen.

Corrine watched him leave as rage replaced the tears. *I hate that man. I hate this place and the company he keeps.*

Corrine got the sourdough pot from the shelf by the stove, flour, sugar, salt, rendered bear fat, and baking soda. As she mixed the ingredients, her mind began to wonder.

Jack doesn't work for him anymore? What does that mean? Did he quit? Did Papa fire him? Perhaps something happened to him? The one person she could call a friend was gone.

Her left cheek felt feverish, like her little brother had felt all over when he died from the white man's flu. He was only three winters old. She was six. But that was long ago.

Why think of him now? And, what did Papa mean by, 'I may end up like her'? Did my mother stand up to him like I just did? she wondered.

Or was she so despondent and downtrodden that she took her own life in the Yukon? Corrine had always wondered about that, even as a little girl. *No! She would never do something like that.*

The one thing Corrine remembered the most about her mother was that she was a strong woman. *She had to be to put up with the likes of him.*

So, if he thought she was like her mother, well then, she took that as a compliment.

As the biscuits baked, she replenished what she had taken out of the sourdough pot with equal parts of flour and water and a little sugar. She'd learned long ago the importance of keeping the sourdough pot full and bubbling.

Again, she heard the kitchen door open. Her eyes followed the sound. Frank Ward and his grin walked in. A thought flashed through her mind. *Maybe I can get some information out of him.*

"Now what?" she asked, as she looked back down at her work.

"The boss told me to check on the biscuits."

She looked him in the face. She knew that her cheek was still red and that her eyes were probably puffy from the crying. "Give 'em five more minutes."

Frank Ward's grin disappeared. "Are you alright?"

"No, I'm not alright. But I can handle it," She watched his jaws tighten. *Now I have him where I want him.* "Ward?"

"Yes?"

"Where's Jack?"

Ward took a deep breath, looked down to the floor, and said, "I know how much you liked him. The only time I saw you smile was when he was around, so it pains me to tell you this. A grizzly mauled Jack. He's dead."

Again, tears welled up in her eyes. This time, tears of sorrow and grief.

"Don't tell the boss I told you, ya hear? Or we'll both be in trouble," Ward turned to leave the kitchen.

Corrine forced herself to stop crying as she searched for a clean rag. Finding one, she rinsed it in cold water and held it to her face. The heat from the oven and the heat from the slap slowly faded away. She dried her face, checked the biscuits, and found that they were done.

Corrine carried the big Dutch oven full of stew out to the table and placed it in the middle. When she returned with the biscuits, half the stew was gone and the only sounds were the tapping of spoons on the metal bowls, slurping, and grunts of contentment.

She returned to the kitchen and sat down, dog-tired.

I need to get out of here.

But where would she go? She had no family and no friends either, for that matter. Her last relative was her mother's father, Black Wolf, one of the elders in Fort Yukon. He died two winters ago.

No, she decided. *I'll have to figure something else out.*

CHAPTER 3

J ust as the sun peeked through a partly cloudy sky over the Alaska Range that made up the southern horizon, Dalton stepped into the clearing in the willows where he'd found Yukon Jack.

The clearing, such as it was, was made by the willows having been uprooted or snapped off at the base by the fight Jack had with the grizzly. The light skiff of snow was not quite enough to cover sign of other human activity in the clearing, and Dalton's sharp eyes, practiced by years of tracking man and beast, quickly picked it out.

Looks like somebody else has been here, he mused. *Why didn't they help him? How long did he lie here before I found him?*

Dalton moved the snow around with the toe of his boot, looking for Jack's rifle or anything else he could find. At first, he found only bits of torn clothing, bear hair, and blood. At the edge of the clearing, a glint of steel caught his eye. Dalton squatted down, brushed the snow aside, and revealed a fixed-blade sheath knife covered in blood and grizzly hair.

This must be the knife he used. Then, looking around, he said to no one, "Fought back pretty good from the looks of things."

Dalton picked up the knife, wiped it with snow to clean off the blood, and stowed it in his pocket.

Looking up, he noticed a trail of blood spatters through some of the standing willows and realized the bear had probably gone through there when it left. Jack had said he thought he had stabbed the bear in the jugular vein and from the looks of it, he probably did. That meant the bear couldn't be too far off.

Dalton stood and followed the blood trail through the willows toward the river. When he broke out of the willows, he found himself standing at the edge of the gravel bar facing the inside bend of the river.

The snow had covered the blood-splattered trail, so he brushed the snow away in a semi-circle, and found the crimson red drops turned right and headed downstream. Dalton walked in that direction, pausing every few feet to brush the snow away to see if he was still on track.

When he reached the end of the gravel bar, he realized he had been hearing ravens; Alaska's version of the vulture. Dalton listened, watched, and soon saw three of them sitting in a tree across the river a few yards from the bank. He knew where the bear was.

The big, black ravens "cawed" their protest and flew from tree to tree as Dalton waded the river and made his way up the bank. They began their work by pecking the eyes out of the old boar, for indeed that is what he was.

Upon inspection, Dalton found the bear's teeth were worn down. One lower canine tooth was broken off, leaving a nasty cavity which must have hurt. He was scarred from many a fight in his long life.

Dalton found a fresh bullet wound in the left shoulder. When he opened the bear up, he found the bullet lodged in the bone. It wasn't fatal, but it probably pissed the bear off. Dalton confirmed that what did kill him was Jack's knife severing the jugular vein.

Dalton thought about salvaging some of the meat but the bear had been dead for at least a couple of days and the thick hide and fur had held the body heat in. The meat was already tainted.

"Well, at least you ravens will have food for a while," he said to the coal-black bird watching him from a nearby tree.

The raven stared at him blankly, ruffled its feathers, and preened himself. Faintly amused by the birds, Dalton smiled to himself, turned, and headed back to camp.

***

With an armload of firewood, Dalton stepped out of the shadows and into the warm glow of a dying campfire. It surprised him to find Bandit lying next to Jack and allowing him to pet her.

"She must like you. Like me, she doesn't normally trust other people," he said as he put the wood down and poked at the few remaining live coals.

Jack looked at Dalton with his one good eye and said with his raspy voice, "She reminds me of a dog the Malamute Kid used to have."

"The Malamute Kid?"

Jack cleared his throat and said, "Yeah, the real one. The one Jack London modeled his character after in his book. He was, and still is I suppose, the best dog-driver I've ever known. I used to run mail with him up in Circle City. Say, I sure could use a drink of water."

Dalton helped Jack sit up and lean against the spruce. He could see that this poor old sourdough was in a lot of pain, but Jack did not say a word. Dalton handed him his canteen and watched as Jack pulled two long slugs of water from the spout then hand it back.

"Thanks, I was gettin' dry."

Dalton put the canteen away, laid a pile

of small, dead, dry twigs from under a spruce on the coals, and blew them into a flame. He added bigger sticks, then sat back against another spruce and dug through his pack for some smoked salmon. Squaw candy, as some folks call it.

He broke off a chunk, handed it to Jack. "Here, have some breakfast, if you think you can hold it down. So, you've been around awhile, I take it?"

"Thanks. Yeah, I guess so. I was one of them fools that had a lust for gold in '98. Climbed the Chilkoot with the rest of those misfits and made a good chunk of change that first year. The second year, my claim began to peter out so I sold it and headed back to the states.

"When I got back, my folks were having a hard time making ends meet. I couldn't stop thinking about this country though, so I gave them the money and headed north again. Started delivering mail from Dawson to Circle City where I met the Kid."

Dalton broke off a chunk of the dried salmon, fed it to Bandit. "That got ya to Canada. What brought ya to Fairbanks? The gold strike, like everyone else?"

Jack remained silent for a moment as he chewed on the salmon. "That, and the desire to see new country. I love this land. I reckon I'll die here in the north. Darn near did, too,

I guess. Much obliged for your help. By the way, what did you say your name was?"

"Dalton Laird."

Jack stopped chewing with his mouth half open, then quickly closed it. He looked away then back at Dalton, swallowed. "I've heard of you. You have quite a reputation in these parts. Folks say you bring in the best furs anyone has ever seen. They say you really understand animals, and wolves in particular."

Dalton thought he detected something in Jack's reaction that went unsaid. Something Jack didn't want to reveal. Whatever it was, Dalton dismissed it, for now.

"I make it my business to handle the furs as best I can. I think they deserve it. After all, they make my living for me. I figure I'm like a farmer. I try to take the surplus and leave seed for next year. If I over-harvest all the furs this year, I won't have any next year."

"That makes sense, I guess. But how do you know when you're taking the surplus and when you're taking the seed?"

"I keep records of my catches. If I find I'm taking more females than males, I'll pull my traps and move somewhere else. As far as the wolves are concerned, they interest me the most, I guess. I caught a young, black male pup a couple of winters ago and bred him with one of my better females. Bandit here is the result."

"Well, ya must be doing something right," Jack said. "She's a right smart dog."

Silence grew between the two for a moment, and then Jack asked, "What about you? What brought you to God's country?"

Dalton sat quiet for a moment. He gazed into the fire, remembering while trying to keep the flood of emotion contained. Even now, after all these years, it still hurt.

"The love of a woman. Or more correctly, the lack thereof. I thought we were the perfect couple, only to find out her love for me was a devil's lie. So, I gave her the divorce she wanted and came up here to get away from it all. To live life on my own terms. There's a lot more to it than that. I won't bore ya with the details. Let's just say I don't trust women much anymore."

"I guess trailing a woman's heart can be full of all kinds of danger."

Dalton smiled and said matter-of-factly, "I think women, in general, are dangerous, not just their hearts...So, tell me what you remember about the attack."

"Well, I was makin' my way through the willows to the river. Just as I stepped out of the willows, I saw that griz on the sand bar, eating the rotting carcasses of spawned out salmon. He must have caught my scent 'cause he looked up just as I turned to head back through the willows. That near-sighted brute must've thought I was a calf moose or something 'cause he lit out for me as fast as he could.

"I panicked and ran for the trees but he caught me in the willows. Just as he caught up to me, I jumped to the side and smacked him with the butt of my rifle on his head. His momentum carried him on a few feet past me and as he turned to come at me again, I put a bullet in his shoulder hoping to put him down. It didn't.

"Next thing I knew, I was on my back and he was standing over me with my head in his jaws. I could hear a crunching, ripping noise and I thought he had busted my skull. I remember thinking, 'Now, this is a heck of a way to die.'

"I guess it was just his teeth scraping along my skull. Then he stood up with my head still in his jaws and shook me like a rag doll. I guess my scalp ripped loose and he dropped me. I landed on my stomach and he bit me in the right leg a couple of times. I tried to play dead but the next thing I knew I was on my back again. I guess that's when he clawed my side, turning me over.

"Anyway, I had lost my rifle somewhere, but luckily, my knife was still in the sheath. As I grabbed it, he came at my face with his mouth wide open, and I buried that knife to the hilt in the side of his throat.

"Blood went everywhere and he made a strange gurgling sound. He jerked the knife out of my hand as he spun around and ran off."

They both fell silent, chewing on their fish. Dalton wanted to ask about the others who were obviously with him after the mauling but decided against it. He figured Jack would tell him in his own good time. Besides, he had to get Jack back to the cabin to take better care of his wounds, and then on to Fairbanks and a hospital for proper medical care. That was the biggest issue to deal with right now. The rest would come later.

Dalton remembered the knife he'd found in the clearing. He handed it to Jack.

"Found your knife. It was lying next to the willows the bear ran through."

Jack's one good eye widened and a slight smile crossed his face.

"Thanks. I hated to lose it. It belonged to my dad. It means a lot to me."

"Ya feel like traveling? I got a line cabin about four miles upstream on Ninetyeight Creek. We can re-supply there and change your dressings. Besides, from the looks of it, there's a storm coming in. Hopefully, it will dump enough snow to make travel easier into Fairbanks."

Jack winced as he took a deep breath. He tried to suppress a couple of coughs while clutching his side evidently from the pain of the bruised or cracked ribs. "I hate to be a burden to ya, Mr. Laird, but I'd be mighty obliged for the help."

Dalton, taken aback by this unexpected show of respect, paused a bit. "My friends call me Dalton."

"Thank you...Dalton."

"I'm sure you would've done the same for me. Now, how's your leg this morning?"

"Feverish, swelled up and stiff. I think I can put some weight on it, though."

Dalton rolled up what was left of the fish in the waxed paper and put it back in the pack, found his Copenhagen and took a dip. Digging through his pack, he took out his small hatchet and fashioned a crutch from the root end of a toppled-over spruce sapling.

"Here, use this and lean on me. We're going to have a tough time getting you back to the cabin."

CHAPTER 4

The combined musky-sweet odor of overripe high-bush cranberries and the damp forest floor lay heavy in the air. Big, thirsty snowflakes fell as the two men broke camp in preparation for their journey upstream. They traveled under the canopy of spruce as there was less snow, but in the trade off they dealt with thorny wild rose bushes.

Six long hours later, they struggled to the cabin door through a foot of new snow. Once inside, Dalton helped Jack onto the bunk and then started a fire in the stove. He put on a dishpan-full of creek water to heat then went outside and climbed the ladder of his cache.

Dalton rummaged around inside the cache for extra clothes and some meat from the hindquarter of a cow caribou he had killed and smoked a couple of weeks earlier.

Back inside the cabin, Dalton put the meat on the table and handed the clothes and a bar of soap to Jack.

"When the water's hot enough, wash up as best you can. If any of these clothes fit, you're welcome to 'em. I'll fix us something to eat."

Within a few minutes, steam rose from the pan. Dalton placed the warm water and a rag on the table and pulled it close to Jack so he could reach it.

Jack reached for the rag and sighed deeply.

"What's wrong?" Dalton asked.

"I feel like I'm such a burden to you. I wish there was some way to pay you back for all you've done," Jack said as he dipped the rag into the warm water.

"Well, I hope you would've done the same for me. I guess there are some men in this country who are only here to feed their greed and lust. They take what they can and move on. Those men wouldn't give a nickel for another man's life." Dalton noticed Jack's jaws tighten. "Wanna tell me about it?"

Jack wrung the rag out over the steaming water, held it to his face for a few moments, enjoying the warmth of it. He wiped his face, gingerly dabbing at the stitches and his swollen eye. Then he wrung the bloody rag out in the water again. He steadied his one-eyed gaze on Dalton.

"Those sons-a-you-know-whats left me to die, Dalton. Can you believe that? They left me to die."

"Kinda figured that's what happened. I saw signs of other people there. You know, footprints and disturbed snow you or the bear couldn't have made. Who were they?"

"Jon Batiste's crew."

"Who's he?"

"He's one of them you just described. He's here to get all he can and then get out. And God help you if you stand in his way. He started a company he calls the Interior Syndicate. He's trying to control interest in mining and furs. Mostly furs, since the mining has slowed down and the price of furs has gone up. He wants to start a fur company."

Jack rinsed out the rag in the hot water, wrung it out, then held it to his swollen eye again.

"Well, there's nothing wrong with starting a fur company, I guess." Dalton carved a couple of steaks from the caribou meat.

"Not in-and-of itself, I agree. But I'm tellin' ya, this guy is sinister. Batiste's got visions of grandeur. I heard tell that his grandpappy was the factor at the Fort Yukon post for the Hudson Bay Company years ago before the government convinced them they were on U.S. soil. He wants to start something like that up again. He's hired a bunch of trappers to get all the furs they can, by hook or by crook. I never did feel right about workin' for him.

I tell ya, I'm kinda glad I ran into that bear. At least it gave me an out."

Dalton put a dollop of bacon grease in a hot skillet on the stove, then added the steaks. "What do you mean, it gave you an out?"

"Well...I guess it means they think I'm dead. I can get away from 'em without 'em coming after me. Batiste's got a tight grip on that gang of his and if you do anything to cross him, the Lord help ya."

"So, what were ya all doing out here?"

Jack dipped the bloody rag in the steaming water, wrung it out, and then gingerly dabbed the stitches on his head.

"Well, it's no secret in town about the quality and abundance of furs coming out of the Salcha Valley, so Batiste decided to push into this country and lay claim to it. I hired on a few days ago as a hunter to provide meat. I swear I didn't know the Salcha was your huntin' grounds."

Dalton seasoned the steaks with garlic salt and dried onions and pepper then turned them over in the skillet. He watched them sizzle.

He slowly shook his head as he processed what Jack told him. A man like Batiste had no regard for human life. Dalton had had dealings with crooks like this Batiste fella' in his past life as a Deputy Sheriff back in the states. Back when his marriage failed and everything fell apart. The only thing Dalton wanted was to be left alone and live an independent, self-sufficient life. Now, some yaw-hoo wanted to move in and push him out of this valley. His valley. Well, he was not about to let that happen. Besides, how could anyone with a conscience leave someone to die in the bush without trying to help? That was kin to murder in Dalton's book.

"I just don't understand why someone would go off and leave a wounded man in the bush to die," Dalton said.

"That's just the kind of men they are. I remember lying there after the attack, drifting in and out of consciousness and hearing them discussing what to do. I vaguely remember hearing Batiste say, 'Let him lay. He's so tore up, he wouldn't make it back to Fairbanks anyway. He'll die soon enough.'

"Next thing I know, it's getting dark and I can hear them leaving. A few of them are talking and I hear Frank Ward say, 'Grab his rifle. He won't be needin' that anymore. And gather up his gear. We may need some of that stuff.' And then they were gone.

"I drifted in and out all that night and yesterday, and then last night you found me."

"So, who's this Frank Ward fella?" Dalton handed a plate with one of the steaks to Jack. Jack took it and placed it on the table in front of himself.

"Jon's right-hand man, I guess you could call him. Jon's business associate. I never liked him much."

"The name sounds familiar, but I can't place it." Dalton placed a knife and fork near Jack's plate.

Jack's bruised hand gingerly handled the knife as he cut off a chunk of meat and stuffed it in his mouth. When he had it half-chewed, he said, "Some folks say he used to hang out with the Blue Parka Bandit when he robbed miners and stages along the roads in Goldstream Valley, back about aught five."

"Aw, that's where I heard the name. He was never convicted though, from what I remember."

"Nope, never was. The weasel got out of it." Jack's face wore a look of disgust, then brightened. "Dadgum-it-all but this tastes good. But then, a wolverine would taste good about now."

After supper, Dalton helped Jack lay back on the bunk. Dalton went outside and dug the roots of some fireweed near the cabin. Back inside the cabin, he cleaned the roots and placed them in a wooden bowl. He mashed them into a poultice for Jack's wounds. He recalled the Athabaskan people claimed raw fireweed would draw pus from wounds and would stop the wound from closing up so that it could drain properly. Then, on second thought, he added a good dose of salt to the batch. He figured if the fireweed didn't work, the salt probably would. He searched the shelf above the window and found some gauze. Dalton turned his attention to Jack.

"Jack. Wake up."

Jack jumped a little, rolled his head and fixed his one good eye on Dalton. "I was just sneakin' up on a full curl ram."

Dalton smiled to himself. "Let's get you doctored up and re-wrap your wounds with this poultice. Then you can have all night to stalk that beast."

"Alright. If you say so."

After Dalton finished re-wrapping Jack's wounds, he put away the supplies and sat down at the table.

After a moment of silence, he said, "Jack, I've got to get you to a doctor in Fairbanks. There's no two ways about it. But first, I've got a twelve-mile hike over to the South Fork of the Chena. There's another trapper over there that's taking care of my dogs. I should be back tomorrow. About noon at the earliest. You think you'll be alright while I'm gone?"

"Yeah, don't worry 'bout me none." Jack sat up a bit in the bunk. "But that's quite a hike. You've already put in, what...over twenty miles today? Besides, what time is it? Eight o'clock, or so? You need some rest your own self."

"Twenty-five miles, and it's nine o'clock. But we have no time to waste. Barring any problems, and if I leave now, I'll get there about two in the morning, catch about four hours of sleep, then head back with the dogs.

"There's plenty of wood by the stove and the water bucket's full. Just relax and get some rest until I get back."

"Well...if I can't change your mind, luck to ya on the trail, partner."

CHAPTER 5

Dalton and Bandit headed northwest behind the cabin and traveled about two-and-a-half miles up Ninetyeight Creek. The newly fallen snow reflected enough ambient light Dalton easily picked out the trail. That, along with Bandit's unerring leader instincts kept them on course.

When they came to the right fork, they followed it about six miles then turned left and climbed a pass in the hills. Once on top, Dalton could look down into the headwaters of the South Fork of the Chena River. Turning left, they followed the ridge line northwest about three miles, which gradually descended to Ollie Olson's cabin.

Dalton checked his pocket watch. "Two-fifteen, Sunday morning. I figured that pretty close," he said aloud. Remembering the north woods etiquette of announcing your presence, he hollered, "HELLO, THE CABIN!"

Instantly the dogs raised a ruckus.

Dalton hollered two more times and was about to holler again when the cabin door opened and light spilled onto the snow.

"WHO GOES DERE?" a voice called back.

"DALTON, DALTON LAIRD."

"YUMPIN' YIMMINY. COME ON IN."

Dalton made his way the last few yards to the cabin. His dogs had recognized his voice. They whined and jumped up and down, straining at the end of their chains. Dalton couldn't help but laugh at their antics. Then, he threw back his head and howled like a wolf. Instantly, the dogs answered back with a chorus of wolf and husky howls of their own.

"Alright, alright. Settle down, you bunch of good-for-nothing mixed breed curs."

"It look like dey miss you, shore nuff." Ollie laughed.

"Yeah, well, I missed them too. They're the only things that put a smile on my face nowadays it seems." Dalton waded in among the dogs and petted each one.

"What bring ya back so soon? I figured you be gone t'ree week or so."

"Ollie, I'm sorry for wakin' ya in the middle of the night like this, but I got my hands full and time is of the essence. I'd be glad to tell ya all about it. But first, I need to get off my feet. I'm bushed."

"Sure t'ing. Come on in."

A half hour later, and after Dalton had told him everything that had happened, Ollie took a couple of thoughtful puffs on his pipe.

"You yust be careful dis Batiste fella, ya hear? I heard plenty bad t'ings about him. My voman's people say he cheat dem plenty bad when they trade fur."

"Why don't they just sell their furs to the Northern Commercial Company or somebody else? They don't have to trade to Batiste."

"Batiste, he make it easy for dem. He and his men travel to da gold camps, villages, and trap lines to trade. That way dey don't have to go to town. Only t'ing is, he give below market value for da furs, and charge too much for da supplies."

"And if they refuse to trade?"

"He take da fur anyway. Last winter, dey say his men killed a couple of deir people when dey refused to trade with him."

"Really?"

"Yep."

Dalton sat silent, thoughtful, reflecting on what Ollie had told him. Then Ollie said, "I need to go to da John, den bring in an armload of firevood. I'll be back in a few."

"Take your time. I need to do some thinkin' anyway."

As Ollie left the cabin, Dalton took a sip of coffee and decided that this Mr. Jon Batiste was an ambitious man and a killer. A man like him who has killed once will kill again. Dalton had seen it before. Moreover, to Dalton, it didn't matter if the victim was Indian or white, murder was murder. Batiste was also a man who liked to have other men of questionable integrity work for him.

Take Frank Ward for instance. Some say he was in cahoots with Charles Hendrickson, the Blue Parka Man, working as a highwayman along the roads to the gold camps in the Goldstream Valley and the Chatanika. The Blue Parka Man was caught by Deputies Dreibelbis and Wiseman, convicted, and sent to prison in the States.

Ward, on the other hand, was nowhere to be found. It was rumored that two or three miners who could've identified Ward as one of the bandits had mysteriously died in cabin fires or cave-ins in their drift mines. No one could ever prove Ward had anything to do with their deaths.

Now, after five years of silence, Ward shows up with Batiste, forms a company called the Interior Syndicate and starts trying to control interests in mining and furs.

Well, the miners are too well-organized to let that happen, he decided. Besides, gold production had dropped from $10.5 million last year, to about $6.1 million this year. From the looks of things, the trend was going to continue. The trappers, on the other hand, that was a different story.

Being more independent-minded, trappers weren't organized at all. With fur prices as good as they have been the last few years, and if Batiste could trap out and steal most of the fur in the Tanana River Basin, he stood to make quite a bit of money. But how would he do it? Trapping and trading would take too long. That would require a lot of manpower.

No, he has something else in mind, he told himself.

Dalton mulled this over in his head and was about to take a sip of coffee when Ollie burst through the cabin door with an armload of stove wood. Dalton placed the tin cup on the table, then got up and closed the door behind Ollie. He watched Ollie dump the wood into the wood box by the stove and brush the sawdust and debris from the front of his parka. Then Dalton realized he'd not seen Ollie's better half anywhere.

"Say, where is your woman anyway?"

"Oh, she yust running da trap line, cutting vood for da line cabins, gettin' 'em ready for da vinter. She should be back in two, t'ree days."

Dalton looked down at the cabin floor and slowly shook his head.

"You've got yourself one good woman there, Ollie." He looked at Ollie and said, "By the way, what *is* her name, anyway?"

"I don't know. It's too hard to pronounce, so I yust call her my voman. Sometimes I call her Sally." Ollie shed his parka and hung it from a nail sticking out of a cabin log.

Ollie turned and grinned at Dalton with a mouth full of tobacco smoke-stained teeth. Chuckling a little, Dalton asked, "How come I haven't heard of this Jon Batiste fella before?"

Ollie picked up his pipe and knocked the burnt tobacco out of it on the table's edge. "As much of a lone wolf as you are, it's a vonder ya even know Vairbanks exists."

Dalton thought a bit before responding. "I guess you're right. It's just that Fairbanks is getting so big. I feel jittery with so many people around me. But, I intend to go there tomorrow."

"Ya goin' to have a little talk with Batiste?"

"Yeah, I think so. After I get Jack to the doctor. I'm going to try to convince Batiste to stay out of my trapping territory. I've worked too hard to build it up to what it is. And I'll dang sure fight for it."

Ollie slapped his knee and said with a laugh, "Yumpin yimminy! I'd like to see dat, I vould. You yust vatch yerself around him though, ya hear?"

* * *

Three hours later, Dalton awoke and stepped outside to relieve himself. His exhaled clouds of breath slowly drifted away and disappeared like the memories of lives long forgotten.

It was dead calm in that land of snow, and he watched the northern lights weave across the sky like a curtain stirred by a gentle breeze. Up on the ridge, a wolf howled its loneliness for the world to hear. It started with a deep bass note, rose to a high baritone, and then faded away to deep bass again, unlike the high-pitched yipping sound of coyotes Dalton remembered in his youth.

Every time he heard a wolf howl, it sent shivers down his spine and awoke within him some long forgotten stirring civilization could not dispel.

Bandit couldn't contain herself and answered back in her sweet seductive wolf voice. Dalton looked down at her and she up at him. He almost swore he saw a smile on her face.

Dalton smiled. "You hussy."

Ollie insisted Dalton stay long enough for a breakfast of sourdough pancakes, which he did and was thankful, for he had worked up a powerful hunger.

Later, Dalton packed his gear on a packboard with a packsack Ollie loaned him and headed out to the dog yard. He unsnapped the chains on all six dogs to let them run a bit while he put the chains in the pack. Ollie emerged from the cabin and handed Dalton a paper package.

"What's this?"

"More pancakes and squaw candy. It'll do ya till ya get to your place."

"Thanks. And thanks for taking care of my dogs again. I'll settle up with ya after I get a few furs, if that's alright?"

Ollie smiled. "Yust clean Batiste's clock for my voman and her people. Dat'll be payment enough for vatching your dogs."

CHAPTER 6

As Dalton approached his cabin door, he realized there was no smoke rising from the stovepipe. A sense of unease gave way to apprehension as he approached the door. Dalton pulled the latchstring, pushed the door open, stepped inside, and moved to the right, as was his habit. This in effect moved his silhouette out of the door frame and allowed more light into the dark recesses within.

"Jack, you in here?"

Nothing.

As his eyes slowly adjusted, he recognized Jack lying on the bunk. Dalton quickly scanned the rest of the interior then moved to Jack and placed a hand on his forehead. Jack was alive but incoherent and burning up with fever. Dalton realized he couldn't wait until morning. He had to get Jack to town NOW.

Dalton retrieved the sled from the roof of the cache, then harnessed Bandit and clipped her into the tug line first. She pulled the tug line taught while Dalton harnessed and clipped the other dogs into the leads at their turn.

Dalton folded and placed three caribou hides in the bottom of the sled for padding, then he wrapped Jack in his white snowshoe hare blanket and stuffed him into the sled as well, trying to make him as comfortable as possible. He dug around the cache and found his possibles bag he always kept packed with extra clothes, fire starter, and other useful items and lashed it the sled.

Dalton looked around. Satisfied that he had all he needed, he shoved his 30-30 into the gun boot, strapped to the sled, pulled the snow hook that anchored the sled to the ground and yelled, "Hike!"

Instantly, the dogs were pulling for all they were worth. They loved to run and knew adventure awaited them somewhere down the trail.

The biggest problem now was how to get them all across the Salcha to the winter trail on the south bank. Once on the other side, the going would be good. But crossing an unfrozen river without getting too wet was going to be a challenge.

Dalton drove the team upstream about a mile, where the winter trail crossed the Salcha. He found a shallow riffle. He tied the sled to a tree, then picked Jack up and carefully waded across to the other bank. Dalton placed Jack under the overhanging boughs of a spruce.

The trip across was repeated with the rifle, hides, and possibles bag. Again, he waded back to the sled. This time, he untied the sled and drove the dogs across, fast walking beside it to keep it from washing downstream, giving commands to the dogs to slow down.

On the south bank, Dalton tied the sled to a tree so the eager dogs wouldn't run away with it. He sat down, removed his wet boots, socks, and wool pants. He rung out as much water as he could.

After putting his pants back on, he put on dry socks and caribou skin mukluks that were stashed in his possibles bag.

Dalton wasn't too worried about his wet wool pants. He knew fighting to keep the sled upright over the tussocks, and running behind the sled would produce enough body heat to dry his pants out. He packed everything back into the sled basket and they headed south to the Valdez Trail on the banks of the Tanana River at the village of Salchaket, some twenty-three miles away.

When they got to the flats just past where Jack had been mauled, Dalton called the dogs to a halt and stomped the snow hook into a tussock. He and the dogs needed a break to catch their wind. He had run almost as much as the dogs had, fighting to keep the sled upright.

Dalton pulled back the rabbit fur blanket to check on Jack. He was sweating, burning up with fever. Jack needed some air to cool down a bit, so Dalton left the blanket unrolled while he and the dogs rested. Jack had been moaning and mumbling in his delirium every time the sled bounced off a tussock or slammed down going over a log in the trail.

If only there was more snow to even out the bumps. Well, no sense in worrying about that, he decided. *Anyway, once we reach Salchaket, we'll have forty miles of well packed trail on into Fairbanks.*

Twenty minutes later, the dogs were no longer panting and Bandit watched her master for a sign he was ready to go. The dogs were getting restless. Some jumped up and down; others strained against their leads. The seven-mile run from the cabin had loosened up their muscles and they were eager to travel.

Dalton patted each one on the head and checked their feet to make sure there were no injuries. When he got to Bandit, he checked her over closely, then knelt in front of her and gave her a hug.

"Bandit, we got to get this old sourdough to town. Help me keep this team in line." Bandit licked him on the face. Dalton smiled. "Good girl."

Dalton pulled his mittens on while he walked back to the sled and stood on the runners. Stepping on the brake board, he bent down, pulled the snow hook out of the tussock, and stowed it in the holster lashed to the handlebar. One quick look over the team to make sure no lines were crossed, he gave the command, "Hike!" Instantly the seven dogs pulled strong. A hundred yards down the trail, they settled into a ground-eating pace.

Two hours later, just at sunset, a chorus of howls and barking from the dog yard of William Munson's Roadhouse in Salchaket greeted Dalton and his dog team as he stood on the brake.

An Indian helper ran up from the dog barn to Dalton's sled. Dalton set the snow hook as best he could and lifted Jack out of the basket. Dalton heard the door of the Roadhouse open and a baritone voice say, "Come on in, stranger. Got hot grub waitin'. The boy there, Jimmy, can take care of your dogs."

Dalton held Jack, faced the Indian helper, and said, "Give 'em half rations. I'll be leaving soon and I don't want 'em running on a full belly." Then, he turned and faced the voice, "Bill, I need your help."

Dalton saw the expression on Bill Munson's face change as Bill leaned the rifle he was holding against the wall. "Dalton, where have... what do ya... who have ya got there?"

Dalton took a couple of steps toward the door.

"Says his name's Jack Farley. He's been bear-mauled and burning up with fever."

Munson rushed forward to help Dalton carry Jack inside the Roadhouse. When they got him inside, they laid him on a bed in one of the spare rooms.

The two men watched as Mrs. Munson brought in a pan of cool water and a rag to cool and clean Jack's swollen face.

"Kinda hard to tell, what with the swollen face and stitches, but yeah, I'd say that's Yukon Jack alright," said Munson. "What happened?"

"Found him a couple of days ago, up by my line shack on Ninetyeight Creek. I cleaned and stitched his wounds as best I could.

"He seemed to be doing pretty well when I left him last night at the cabin to get my dogs from Ollie Olson. But when I got back a little after noon today, this is how I found him; unconscious and burning up with fever. I'm taking him into St. Joseph's Hospital."

"Well, you come on into the kitchen here and I'll get ya something to eat. The missus there will look after him. You must be starved."

"Thanks. I am," Dalton said, as they turned to leave the room. Then as an afterthought, "You got some paper and a pencil? I need to write a message for the Army Signal Corps office to let the hospital know we're coming."

"Yeah, I do. Jimmy can run it over there as soon as he takes care of your dogs," Munson led Dalton into the kitchen.

Dalton sat down at the table. "Looks like ya got a new hand."

"Yeah I do. He's a good worker, that boy is." Munson brought Dalton a bowl of stew and a plate of biscuits. He went back into the kitchen and returned with a pot of coffee, a note pad, and a pencil.

Sitting down opposite of Dalton, he poured himself and Dalton a cup. "I hope the Washington Alaska Military Cable and Telegraph System is up. They had some downed lines to contend with recently."

"Really? What happened?" Dalton asked between mouthfuls of food.

"Evidently an amorous bull moose in rut decided to use a couple of telegraph poles to take out his frustrations, a few days ago. Pushed 'em right over."

Dalton smiled and shook his head while chewing his food.

"They should have 'em reset by now, though."

The front door swung open and Jimmy walked in. Munson nodded toward a seat at the table. "Have a seat and some coffee. Mr. Dalton needs you to run a message over to the Signal Corps office in a few minutes."

Jimmy closed the door, removed his parka, and hung it on a nail. He quietly sat down at the table. Dalton scribbled a message on the paper and handed it to the Indian.

Taking the note, Jimmy got up to leave, but Dalton stopped him. "No, no. Sit down and have your coffee. There'll be time to do that later."

Jimmy looked at Munson, who shook his head and nodded to the chair.

As Jimmy sat back down, Munson asked Dalton, "Any idea what he was doing in your neck of the woods?"

Dalton looked up. "Jack? Well, he mentioned he hired on with an outfit called the Interior Syndicate as a meat hunter, run by some guy named Jon Batiste. Evidently, Batiste's trying to build a monopoly in the fur trade, 'by hook or by crook', as Jack put it. Mostly by crook, I'm thinkin'."

"Jon Batiste, huh?" Munson rubbed his chin. "They were in here a few days ago, headed back to Fairbanks. Batiste did most of the talking. There seemed to be a sullen mood amongst the boys. Said they were out hunting and scouting new trapping territory. By way of conversation, I asked him where they'd been. He never would say, just gave vague generalities."

Dalton noticed Munson glance over to Jimmy.

"One of 'em, Ward I think they called him, cuffed Jimmy here upside the head."

"What happened?" Dalton asked.

Munson leaned both forearms on the table, grasped his coffee cup with both hands, and looked into it as if inspecting the contents. Then, he looked up at Dalton.

"I was watching them out the window there when Ward came in the door all in a huff and told me I needed to teach my 'Injun' some manners. I saw what happened.

"Jimmy was helping them with their packs and accidentally dropped one. Ward, a tall skinny, light blond-haired fellow, tried to get Jimmy to apologize. When he didn't, Ward backhanded him across the face."

"Why didn't he apologize?" Dalton asked.

"Jimmy's a mute."

"Didn't you try to explain it?" Dalton asked.

Munson took another sip of coffee, leaned back in his chair and said, "Not with their attitude. Besides, they were all armed pretty heavily. Didn't want to cause any more trouble than necessary."

Dalton took a sip of the strong, hot coffee, stared off into middle space, and thought a bit. Then he set down his coffee cup, took a silver dollar from his pants pocket, and handed it to Jimmy.

"When you're ready, take that message to the Signal Corps. And you can keep that as a tip for your help. I'll get my dogs together."

Jimmy's eyes lit up. He looked at Munson. Munson grinned back at Jimmy and nodded in approval.

Jimmy pushed back from the table, put the coin in his pants pocket, and strode over to the door. After putting his parka on, he neatly folded the message and tucked it safely away in one of the inside pockets and headed out the door.

Mrs. Munson came in from tending to Jack, and Dalton, out of politeness, stood to greet her.

"His temperature is down a little, but he's fighting infection. It'll probably go back up with the stress of trail travel. You need to get him to the hospital as soon as possible, Dalton. And try to keep him cool without frostbite. Don't wrap him up so tight with that blanket, ya hear?"

"Yes ma'am," Dalton said. "I'll do my best."

"I know you will Dalton Laird. I know you will. By the way, young man, when are you going to find a good woman and settle down? Civilize ya a little? Look after ya?"

The question took Dalton totally by surprise and he stammered as he fumbled through his brain for a response. He glanced at Mr. Munson for support, who appeared to be trying not to laugh.

Finally, Dalton blurted out, "Ma'am, I got no room for a woman. Oh, they're pretty and comforting to look at and such, like a campfire at night. But my experience has been that if you get too close, they'll burn ya."

He noticed her countenance slowly change as a frown crossed her face, and he regretted what he had said.

"Dalton, I know your history. Don't judge all women on the actions of a few. Someday you'll look back and wish you hadn't."

Dalton bent over, gave her a kiss on the cheek. "Yes ma'am. I'll keep that in mind. Thanks for supper. You're the best cook this side of the Yukon." He turned to the door, put on his own parka, and headed out to the dog barn.

When Dalton returned with the team, Mr. Munson helped him load Jack in the sled basket. This time Dalton lashed Jack in to minimize movement from the swaying and jostling of the sled.

"It's kinda dark, but the moon's almost full," Munson stated matter-of-factly.

Dalton took out his Copenhagen, took a pinch, and then replaced the can back in his pocket.

"Yeah, I know. But I'm hoping there will be enough light to see. I hope I don't run into one of those rutting bull moose that like to push over telegraph poles."

Dalton slipped on his mittens. Pulling the snow hook, he stashed it in the holster.

"Wish us luck."

CHAPTER 7

About eleven p.m., five hours later, Dalton stood on the brake and stopped the team in front of St. Joseph's Hospital. He tied the sled to the steps and banged on the front door.

The Sisters of Providence had received Dalton's telegram and waited with a litter to help him carry Jack into one of the rooms. The doctor had not yet arrived. Dalton briefly explained what had happened, what he had done, and that he would settle with them later. Dalton then drove the dogs south of town along Cushman Street to a dog livery.

He and the dogs were pretty worn out when Dalton pulled the sliding barn door open enough to get the team and sled through. Most of his dogs were limping. Their pads were tender after lying around most of the summer with nothing to do, then suddenly put into service with a sixty plus mile run. Dalton felt sorry for them.

Dalton pulled the door shut just as Ed, the proprietor, who had been asleep in the back room, came out holding a lantern and a Colt Peacemaker. With a slight Australian accent he asked, "Who's there?"

Dalton turned to him. "Hey Ed. It's me, Dalton Laird. Just got in. Didn't mean to frighten ya."

Ed stuffed the pistol into the front of his pants, then strode over to Dalton and hung the lantern on a post. "No worries, mate. It's getting to be that time of year when business picks up."

Starting with the dogs closest to the sled, the wheel dogs, Ed helped Dalton unhook the leads, remove the halters, and led the dogs to a rope stretched taut along the back wall with short lines spliced in about every five feet. They snapped the short lines onto the collar of each dog and laid down a fresh bed of straw.

Dalton checked each dog's feet for cuts from ice crystals or sticks in the trail. He found one on one of the swing dogs, just behind the leader. The rest were simply tender to the touch.

"Looks like your dogs are stove-up a bit. I got some liniment I made from spruce pitch, Camphor, and a little beeswax. Good antiseptic and it'll protect their pads for a few days while they heal up."

Dalton straightened up from inspecting the last dogs' feet.

"Sounds good. Chinook there," pointing to one of the swing dogs, "has a cut pad on the right front. Wrap it up to keep dirt out of it, if you would. Feed 'em well and give 'em plenty of water. They're a little dehydrated, too. And, give me a couple of those dried Salmon. I'm taking Bandit with me."

"Sure thing, mate. By the way, haven't seen much of ya lately, ya becoming a hermit?"

Dalton turned his head, and looked at Ed, half-annoyed at the question. "No...people sure been asking me that question, or something like it, a lot lately. I don't like big cities and all the change that's goin' on, is all." Dalton picked up his parka and pulled his 30-30 out of the scabbard lashed to the sled. "Now, if you'll excuse me, me and Bandit are going to the Nordale Hotel."

Ed put up both hands. "Alright, alright, mate. Just makin' conversation, is all."

Dalton turned, headed for the door, and half mumbled under his breath, "Askin' me if I'm becoming some kind of hermit or something. Can't a man just be left alone?"

* * *

Dalton woke with a start to someone banging on his door. Bandit, lying on a throw rug by Dalton's bed, growled a warning.

"Who's there?"

"Hotel clerk. You asked to be woke up at seven thirty?"

Dalton sat up, cleared his throat while rubbing his eyes. "Yeah. Yeah, I guess I did. Thanks." Looking down at Bandit, he said, "Let's go get something to eat."

Dalton washed up, got dressed, then he and Bandit made their way downstairs and out onto First Avenue.

Fairbanks in 1910 was a typical, hastily built gold rush town consisting of log cabins, false-front buildings, and boardwalks. Dirt streets, muddy from the recent snows, directed teams of horses and carts pulled by dogs. Unlike gold rush towns in years past, however, and being only eight years old, Fairbanks had the luxury of electrical power, hot-and-cold running water in some buildings, telephones, flush toilets, and fire hydrants.

Freight consisting of everything from livestock to locomotives was brought in during the summer months on stern-wheelers plying the waters of the Yukon, Tanana and Chena Rivers. Men in high-laced, well-oiled boots thumped along the boardwalks and women paraded around in the latest fashions.

Just as he and Bandit entered the Arcade Cafe at eight a.m., the melodious baritone stern-wheeler whistle, mounted on one of Northern Commercials smokestacks at the power plant, echoed across the Tanana Valley. The tinkling sound of silverware against fine china plates and the low hum of folks in conversation, along with the smells of freshly cooked food and coffee, provided an inviting atmosphere.

Dalton seated himself at a corner table in the back of the cafe, facing the entrance and storefront windows. Bandit settled down by his feet.

"Good morning, Dalton. Back in from the bush for a while?" A waitress approached his table. Dalton looked up and an involuntary groan almost escaped his throat as he recognized her.

"Hi, Citalli. Yeah, came in to take care of some business and maybe get some supplies for the winter." He figured she didn't need to know about Jack.

"Well, it's good to see you. Are you going to be in town long?" She poured him a cup of coffee.

Dalton reached for the full cup. "A couple of days, maybe." Dalton took a deep sip.

A moment of silence, then Citalli asked, "Well, what can I get you for breakfast?"

"How about a couple of eggs and some beef, if ya got any, and some fried tatters. Ya got any sourdough biscuits?"

"Fresh batch." She smiled.

"Give me a couple of them, as well."

"Sure thing." Citalli turned to leave. Then Dalton, remembering Bandit only had those two dried salmon he got from Ed last night said, "Also, fry up another steak for Bandit here, too. Rare."

Citalli looked back. Her smile deepened. "Gotcha. One steak, rare, for Bandit." She turned and walked through the double doors which led to the kitchen.

Dalton had forgotten Citalli worked here. One day, last spring, during a moment of weakness he had let her get too close to him, emotionally. She was sweet on him, he knew so he tried to avoid her, as he did all women when he came to town.

However, he thought, *she'd be a good source of information since she works with the public so much. She's probably seen things... heard things.*

Ten minutes later, she was back with the food. As she placed it on the table, Dalton casually asked with a lowered voice, "Citalli, you know anything about a guy by the name of Jon Batiste?"

She paused, looked at him out of the corner of her eye, and then resumed placing the food on the table. She picked up the coffee pot, glanced into his eyes, and refilled his cup. Dalton wondered if she had heard him as he picked up his fork.

Then, she set down the coffee pot, pulled out a chair from the other side of the table, sat, and in a lowered voice to match his, said, "Only that a lot of folks around here don't take kindly to him. Between the cardsharps at the gambling tables and the girls pinchin' their poke, most of the miners are left with nothing but a headache at the end of the night. And, the ones who are lucky enough to have some gold left over, usually get a sap upside the head when they go outside. They wake up to find their poke gone, and they've got a headache too."

Dalton laid his fork on his plate, picked up his coffee cup and took a sip, and gave what she had said some thought. Then he said, "What about law enforcement. Aren't they doing anything about it?"

Citalli shrugged. "The marshals are too busy out in the gold camps. I don't know about the city constable. Personally, I think he's on Batiste's payroll."

Dalton sat his cup down. *Dirty cops. I always hated dirty cops,* he thought.

"Anything else?" Dalton cut off a chunk of steak and stuffed it in his mouth.

Citalli looked up at the wall as if thinking a bit, then looked back at him.

"The trappers have been talking a lot lately about finding evidence of someone being on their lines... you know, fur missing, things stolen from their cabins, caches being ransacked, things like that. Some are quietly blaming Batiste, but most aren't saying a thing. They're afraid of his men, I think."

Dalton finished chewing the piece of steak, swallowed, and then repeated, "Anything else?"

"Well, I think he owns a few girls in the red-light district over on Fourth and Cushman, but that's just speculation on my part. You got dealings with him?"

Dalton took another sip of coffee. "Yeah, I got dealings with him, alright. What's the name of the saloon?"

"Calls it the Amanita. It's a red building with white trim, over on Third Avenue. Can't miss it."

The Amanita huh? Well, that's appropriate, Dalton mused as he took another sip of coffee. *A red mushroom with white spots. Pretty to look at, but deadly poison if you mess with it.*

Citalli stood, reached across the table, and touched Dalton's sleeve. "I get off at three. Come by and see me. You know where I live."

Dalton nearly spilled his coffee as her words jolted him back to reality. "Um...I um, I've got a lot to get done today. Thanks, anyway."

"Well, you're always welcome. Stop by anytime." Then, looking deeply into his eyes, she said, "I've missed you." Citalli turned and walked back into the kitchen.

Dalton closed his eyes, took a deep breath, and let out a long sigh. He opened his eyes, looked at Bandit, who was panting and looking back up at him.

"Doesn't she know I have no room for a woman in my life?" Dalton asked. "All they ever do is cause pain anyway."

Bandit stopped panting and cocked her head sideways.

Dalton smiled. "Never mind."

He finished his breakfast, paid the tab, and stepped out onto the boardwalk with Bandit at his side. Looking down to her, he said, "How about we go take a look at the Amanita Saloon?"

CHAPTER 8

It was dark inside the Amanita when Dalton and Bandit walked through the door. He stepped to the side and waited a bit to let his eyes readjust from the bright glare of the snow outside to the dingy interior of the building.

A quick glance around revealed an ordinary saloon. An old ragtime piano that had seen its better days in Dawson stood at Dalton's right hand, facing the front wall. A stairway along the right wall led up to a balcony and presumably rooms.

Three miners sat at a table by the stairs, openly eying him. Low, muffled voices came from somewhere at the other end of the large room.

A bartender cleaned and put away glassware behind the bar to Dalton's left. As Dalton approached the bartender, the bartender asked, "What can I do for ya, friend?"

"You can tell me where to find Jon Batiste."

The muffled voices from the back of the room silenced. Dalton noticed the muscles of the man's mouth tighten as he nodded sideways, indicating the back of the room.

Dalton turned and walked toward a table in the back where six men were seated or standing, all eyes on him and Bandit. As Dalton moved toward them, he scanned their faces and decided they were indeed a bunch of ruffians.

At the head of the table and with his back to the wall, a short, stocky man sat. Behind the man stood a tall, lanky blond fellow with square jaws and a hat pulled so low his eyes were barely visible. From Munson's description, Dalton surmised him to be Frank Ward. He was lean and all muscle—a scrapper, a street fighter. Dalton knew Ward would be the one to watch.

Behind Ward was a door marked PRIVATE. To the left of that was a set of bat-winged doors leading to what Dalton figured was the kitchen.

As Dalton approached the table, the six men gathered around in a half circle behind the short stocky man—for which Dalton was thankful. At least there would be an obstacle between him and them should things go south.

Dalton stopped on the other side of the table, Bandit to his left.

In a slight French accent, the short stocky man addressed Dalton. "*Bon Jour*. I'm Jon

Batiste and these gentlemen are my associates. What can I do for you?"

"My name's Dalton Laird and I ..."

"Dalton Laird, huh? I've heard of you, no? Have a seat."

Irritated about being cut off in mid-sentence, Dalton intentionally put an edge to his voice.

"Like I was saying, I would like to talk to ya..." then with a quick glance at the other men, "...in private."

Batiste's eyes narrowed a bit.

"*Non*! As I said, these gentlemen are my associates. You can say whatever you have to say in front of them."

"Alright Batiste, if that's the way ya want it, I'll lay it out on the table. Stay out of my trapping territory 'cause I'll fight ya for it."

Batiste smiled, then laughed. The other men joined in, laughing at Dalton.

"There's no... how you say, beating around the bush with you is there? I like that." Then Batiste stopped smiling, leaned forward, and with a scowl on his face said, "You're a fool, Dalton. There's no law that says I can't trap anywhere I want."

One of the men inched around to Dalton's right. Bandit slipped behind Dalton and met him with a low wolf growl. The man stopped, frozen in place, eyes fixed on Bandit.

Dalton half-turned his head to the man. "I wouldn't do that, if I were you."

The man glanced at Batiste. Batiste gave the man a look as if to say, you idiot, and gave him a nod to get back in line, which he did.

Dalton turned his attention back to Batiste. "Maybe not. But there are unwritten laws of common decency here in the Northland."

"In case you haven't noticed, hiding out in the bush as you do, Mr. Laird, the North is changing. Big business is taking over. Miners are selling out to corporations for big money. Fur prices are on the rise and I'll do anything I can to get my share of the wealth."

Dalton clenched his teeth and leaned forward. His fists crashed onto the table. "Does that include killing a poor Indian for his pelts? Does that include the callous disregard for human life by leaving a man behind to suffer and possibly die?"

The look of shock which crossed Batiste's face inwardly pleased Dalton. He watched Batiste's eyes widen, as Dalton's words registered in Batiste's brain. "He's alive?"

Dalton half-smiled at the satisfaction of knowing he had just counted verbal coup on this man and made Batiste tip his hand. "Yeah. He's alive."

In his peripheral vision, Dalton noted Ward moving behind the line of men, working his way to Dalton's right.

Batiste's face turned red and a vein in his neck pulsed. Batiste opened his mouth, about to say something when someone emerged from the kitchen.

Dalton glanced up and did a double take as he realized a beautiful young woman stood before him. He noticed the pupils of her hazel eyes grow wide as their eyes locked, and then she quickly looked away. Her long, chestnut hair brought forth the vision of a wild stallion running across the planes; every move with grace and purpose. Dalton couldn't help but stare.

Batiste half-turned toward the girl, and with anger and a little more volume than necessary said, "Corrine, get back in that kitchen!"

Corrine took a couple of steps backward, glanced up at Dalton, turned, pushed the bat-wing doors and disappeared behind them.

Turning back to Dalton, Batiste said, "As far as I'm concerned, this discussion is over. Ward, show him the door."

"My pleasure, Boss." Frank Ward took another step toward Dalton.

Dalton straightened up and faced Ward. "Mister, you lay a hand on me and you will live to regret it."

The coldness in Dalton's voice, the fire in his eyes, and the wolf-like growl that rumbled from deep inside Bandit's chest stopped Ward in his tracks.

Dalton held his gaze for a few seconds, then turned back to Batiste. "You just remember what I said."

Batiste and Dalton glared at each other. Batiste pointed at the door. "Ward, get him out of here, NOW!"

Ward, with new resolve, took three more steps toward Dalton and pulled a knife from his waistband.

Before Dalton could react, Bandit lunged at Ward and crushed down on the wrist that held the knife.

Ward screamed in pain. He switched the knife to his left hand and slashed at Bandit, slicing her right shoulder.

She released Ward as she yelped.

Infuriated, Dalton leapt into action. He stepped in with a quick left to Ward's jaw.

The blow stunned Ward. Dalton wrested the knife free with his right hand. With his left hand, Dalton lifted Ward up by the collar and slammed him down on the table.

Everyone cleared away. Ward's head bounced on the table and knocked his hat off.

Dalton raised the knife, contemplated pinning Ward's head to the table, then stabbed the knife into the table, clipping Ward's left ear. Ward froze.

Dalton glared into Batiste's eyes.

"Let this be a warning."

CHAPTER 9

Limping from the wound, Bandit led the way as Dalton backed his way to the door, Dalton kept his eyes on Batiste's men while scanning the rest of the bar. Dalton noticed the miners had cleared out and the bartender stood behind the bar with both hands clearly visible on the counter top, fingers spread, indicating he didn't want any trouble.

When he got Bandit outside, Dalton sat down on one of the chairs on the boardwalk and checked her over. He found the knife wound was not life-threatening, but she did need to have it sewed up. He gave her a hug. "Well, girl, thanks for the help."

She whined softly and licked his face.

Dalton stood, took out his Copenhagen, and took a pinch to settle the effects of the adrenaline dump. "I better get you over to the hospital."

He gently picked her up and carried her down Third Avenue to Cushman Street, then headed north. People pointed at them and whispered to each other.

Dalton wondered what they were saying. True, you don't often see a man carrying a bloody dog down the street, but then, he was only trying to get some help for his lead dog, like anyone else would do.

The miners seated at the table must have cleared out and spread the word about what had happened. News travels fast in a small town.

Well, let 'em talk, he thought. He had other things on his mind.

At First Street, Dalton stopped to take a breather. His arms cramped from carrying Bandit's hundred pounds or so of dead weight. Dalton sat down on a bench on the boardwalk and cradled her in his lap.

Looking around, he noticed a man leaning against the wall of a building he had just passed. The man was not there a minute ago. Now, he was. Dalton filed it away in the back of his mind. While he rested, his thoughts began to wander.

Will Batiste heed my warning?

Batiste did not strike him as a man who was easily persuaded. If anything, being called out in front of his men like that probably strengthened Batiste's resolve.

Well, at least he knows the lay of it. The next move is his to make.

When the cramping subsided, Dalton stood with Bandit still cradled in his arms. He headed for the bridge over the Chena River.

Once on the other side, his arms began to ache again. *No matter. She's more important. And in more pain, too.* Dalton pushed the pain away into the shadows of his mind as he had done all his life, both physically and emotionally.

What about Ward? He had made a fool out of him, too. *Ward will probably come looking for vengeance. And... who the heck was that woman?*

His heart skipped a beat when he thought of her. Other than his first wife, no woman had ever had that kind of effect on him. Dalton shook his head, and tried to clear her image from his brain.

Get her out of your mind, you fool. She'll just muddy up your thinking. She's probably no different than any other woman in your life. Just out to get what they can from you, then leave you for the next sucker to come along.

His arms burned as he climbed the steps of St. Joseph's Hospital. He fumbled with the door and walked in with Bandit.

One of the matronly looking nurses took one look.

"What the...? Get out of here with that dog. This is a HOSPITAL!"

"Exactly. And I want to see the doctor."

The nurse pursed her lips together as if she was going to blow him a kiss, but from the narrowing of her eyes, and the tightening of her jaws, Dalton surmised it wasn't a kiss she was thinking about.

In a steady, lowered tone, she said, "The doctor is busy with a bear-mauling victim..." and then with a raised voice, "NOW, GET OUTSIDE WITH THAT BLOODY DOG!"

Dalton was in no mood for more argument and said in a calm and collected voice, "Ma'am, if you tell me one more time to 'get outside with this dog', I will turn you over my knee."

Dalton saw her eyes open wide and the pursed lips disappear with a gasp. "Well, I never..."

Down the hall, a door swung open and a voice boomed out, "Here now, what's all the noise about?"

Dalton looked past the nurse. "Hey, Doc. I got a bit of a problem here. Can ya help me out?"

A big smile crossed the doctor's face. "Dalton, ya old sourdough. Shoulda known."

The doctor walked up to Dalton and reached out to examine Bandit, but stopped in his tracks when a low rumble of warning came from Bandit.

"It's okay, girl," Dalton said. "The doc will take good care of you."

"Here. Lay her down on this gurney so I can get a better look at her."

Thankful to take the strain off his arms, Dalton placed Bandit on the gurney. He worked the kinks out of his biceps, and then stroked Bandit's head while the doc examined her shoulder.

"Doesn't look like the muscle has been cut. Just a flesh wound. She'll be sore for a few days." Then, over his shoulder, he said, "Nurse, get set up. Looks like we got some suturing to do."

"But, doctor. That's a..."

Dalton saw the doctor turn toward the nurse with a questioning look on his face. "That's a what, nurse?"

"A dog."

"And the best dadgummed lead dog this side of Dawson City, too. Now, do as I say and get set up."

The nurse shook her head and walked away, grumbling under her breath.

The doctor turned back to Bandit then looked at Dalton out of the corner of his eye and grinned.

"Sorry, Doc. I just didn't know what else to do."

"Don't worry about it," The doctor shrugged one shoulder while still looking Bandit over. "There ain't much difference between dogs and humans when it comes to sewing things shut." He turned to Dalton. "If it had been anyone else or any other dog, I might have thought otherwise. Help me roll her in the back room there and I'll get started."

Dalton helped push the gurney to a back room and stood aside as the nurses rushed around in preparation.

While the doc put on his apron, Dalton asked him about Yukon Jack.

"You the one who brought him in here last night?"

Dalton nodded. "Yeah, found him on the Salcha, up by my lower cabin."

Dalton decided the doctor didn't need to know more than was necessary, so he didn't volunteer any more information.

After a three or four second pause, while the nurse helped him put on his rubber gloves, the doctor said over his shoulder, "We got his fever down some, and pumped some fluids in him. He came to this morning. I was in talking to him when you walked in with Bandit."

"Good...good," Dalton said.

The doctor turned to Dalton. He stretched his fingers, getting the tight-fitting gloves settled into place.

"He told me what happened. What he could remember anyway. Said the last thing he remembers was the inside of a cabin. Next thing he knew, he was here."

Dalton watched the nurse apply anesthesia to Bandit. He wasn't really listening.

The doctor took a step closer to Dalton with his gloved hands in the air. "By the way, that was a fine job you did on him considering the conditions you must have been working under. The only thing that concerns me is the infection in his leg. But I have a hunch in a few days he'll be up and walking around. He's a tough old coot."

Dalton smiled and nodded to him once. *Yes. Yes he is.*

"And, one other thing…"

Jeez, does this guy ever shut up? Dalton wondered.

"He'd make somebody a good partner. It's awful dangerous out there alone. And you ain't getting any younger."

Where did that come from? I don't need anybody taggin' along and telling me what to do. Dalton threw a sarcastic smile at the doc. "I'm going to check on Jack."

* * *

Dalton had heard about the hospital since its opening on Thanksgiving Day four years ago. How nice it was with the hot-and-cold running water and flush toilets. He'd never had occasion to check it out himself. That is, until now. He found a room with a toilet. He walked up to it and flushed it.

A smile crossed his face as he watched the water swirl around and go down a small hole in the bottom. He flushed it again.

"Don't that beat all?" He watched the water drain out.

He recalled how the Sisters of Providence, trained in hospital work, had taken charge earlier this year of 1910, and how they ran a tight ship. He decided that probably explained the nurse's frustration with him bringing Bandit inside. But dang it all, Bandit is family.

Dalton walked into Jack's room, pulled up a chair, sat down. "Anything worth reading about?"

Jack, who was reading the Fairbanks Daily Times with his one good eye, said, "Oh, mostly a bunch of nonsense. I guess gold production dropped this year by about four million dollars. They're speculatin' we're seeing the end of the gold rush...Let's see..."

Dalton watched Jack's eye scan down the page a ways, then, with evident surprise in his voice, Jack said, "Evidently Captain Barnette resigned from the Washington-Alaska Bank and pulled completely out of Fairbanks. 'Good riddance,' I say."

Many people in Fairbanks were divided over Captain E.T. Barnette, Dalton knew. Some people said the founder of Fairbanks, an ex-convict, had swindled millions of dollars with his schemes. He had staked claims in the early days on paper only by power of attorney, for relatives, and sold the others to unsuspecting gold rushers for exorbitant sums.

Dalton suspected that Jon Batiste had done, or was doing the same thing. The only difference being Batiste was a small-time operator, more interested in the fur trade and not above taking a life or two in the process.

"Looks like they're makin' plans for another Halloween roller-skatin' party this month." Jack's statement jolted Dalton back to the present.

Dalton grinned at him. "Well, you should be healed up enough by then to go skatin'."

"Danged right, I will. I can't deny the ladies the pleasure of my company. I ain't takin' any of these old nags, that's for sure. You wanna know somethin'? I wanted a Barthel's beer for breakfast and they wouldn't let me have one," Jack wadded up the newspaper and threw it on the floor.

"Yeah, sounds like you're feeling better."

Jack looked at him and they both smiled. Dalton watched as Yukon Jack's smile slowly disappeared. Jack glanced around the room. Dalton realized something important was on Jack's mind.

"Where's Bandit?"

"I got to tell ya, I had a run in with Batiste and his men at the Amanita this morning. It went south in a hurry and Bandit got cut. She's in the other room getting sewed up."

Dalton saw a look of concern cross Jack's face.

"Is she okay?"

Dalton nodded. "She's alright...just a flesh wound. Listen, I don't know if they know you're in here, but the way talk travels in this town, I wouldn't be surprised. I expect a lot more trouble before this thing's over."

"I don't think they'll bother me in here. Anyway, it's my word against his. So, you can count on me to be there for ya. I owe ya one."

Dalton got up, stepped behind the chair, and leaned his forearms on the back.

"Sorry, Jack. I only work alone. And besides, you're all stove up," Dalton studied the floor.

"Look, it's my fault you're in this mess," Jack said with a raised voice.

Dalton looked up at him, "Your fault? What do you mean?"

"If I hadn't got all tore up like this, you wouldn't have had all this trouble I've put you through. You saved my life. I owe you, young'un.

"I got friends in town that can let me know what's going on with Batiste. Yeah, I'm tore up a bit, but I ain't lettin' that stop me. I'll be up and outta here in a few days, mark my words. And like it or not, I'm throwin' in with ya."

Dalton, still leaning on the back of the chair, rocked the chair on its back legs while he mulled over Jack's words.

Standing upright, he looked at Jack and said matter-of-factly, "No, it's not your fault. It's Jon Batiste's fault. One way or another I would have met up with him and we would be right where we are now." Dalton looked out the window and added, "But...I guess I couldn't ask for a better partner."

Dalton's gaze found Jack's eyes again. "I guess you'll do to ride the trail with." And then, he smiled.

CHAPTER 10

Corrine Batiste pulled the wolverine-fur ruff of her smoke-tanned, moose-hide parka more snugly around her throat against the afternoon chill. She noticed more than a few heads turn her way and smiles cross the faces of male passers-by, and the envious and disdainful stares of females as she made her way down the boardwalk.

Most of the white women wore their hair short or rolled up in a bun, but Corrine preferred to wear hers long and straight, sometimes braided as her mother used to. She was accustomed to the attention and paid it no mind. Besides, she had other things on her mind.

She had heard the men talking earlier in hushed tones about whether Dalton had brought Jack into town or not, and if so, which of the two hospitals would he be in. Under the pretense of shopping for kitchen supplies, which her father allowed her to do, she was able to get away to try to find him. She figured she had a fifty/fifty chance of getting it right, so she chose Saint Joseph's and headed in that direction.

Her guess was correct. Corrine gently pushed the door to Yukon Jack's room open just enough to see him lying in bed, propped up, reading a crumpled newspaper. She gently pushed the door open a little more. The door hinge squeaked and caught Jack's attention.

"Miss Batiste, what brings you by?" He grinned and laid the papers down in his lap.

At first, she was repulsed and horrified by the swollen and bruised person that used to be a kindly old man, a man she thought of like a grandfather. She considered running away, but the voice was familiar.

"Miss Batiste, it's alright. It's just me, ol' Yukon Jack." He looked back at the bed he was lying in as if studying the folds of the blanket. "Guess I'm a sight to behold."

Corinne's emotions bubbled up from deep inside and tears filled her eyes. She glided across the room to his bed and took his hand in both of hers.

"I thought you were dead. I noticed you didn't come back with the others and I couldn't get any answers from anybody. I was listening from the kitchen door and then this Dalton person came into the Amanita talking about them leaving someone to die in the bush. And there was a dog and I saw a knife. And then,

Ward landed on the table, and I heard the men talking about you possibly being in the hospital and..."

"Whoa, whoa, whoa girl, slow down. I'm okay. Just got into a tangle with a griz is all."

Corrine squeezed his hand. She squeezed her eyes shut to force out the tears for clearer vision, and force herself to calm down. She was thankful she had not lost the only person left in her life whom she trusted.

"I'm sorry. I'm just concerned. Ward told me you were dead."

Corrine saw Jack's jaws tighten and the little muscle under his ear bulge as he turned and looked out the window. Then he looked back at Corrine and smiled.

"Well, I'm back now. Doc sez I should be up dancing' a jig in a few days. If it wasn't for Dalton, I *would* be dead by now." He nodded his head toward the chair. "Have a seat."

She sensed he didn't want to talk about it or the details, which was okay by her. *Besides,* she thought, *I want to know more about this Dalton Laird.*

"Speaking of Dalton, I've heard people speak the name before. Who is he and what do you think of him?" She sat in the chair Jack offered.

Jack once again looked at his bed, as if studying the folds in the blanket.

"Well...like I said, he saved my life. I only just met him but I think he has a good heart." He looked at Corrine with his one good eye, "From what I've heard, all the old-timers like him. He's pretty much a loner. Doesn't like crowds."

Corrine smiled. "I can understand that. The hustle and bustle of a gold rush town is noisy and it makes *me* nervous. I miss the quiet and solitude of the wild. What else do you know about him?"

Jack looked up at the ceiling, then down the wall as if recalling all the gossip he had heard over the years.

"I recall someone saying he was a lawman back in the states for a couple of years. A Deputy Sheriff, I think." Jack looked at Corrine with his one good eye and a frown upon his face. He watched her for a moment.

Under his steady gaze, Corrine felt a tad uneasy. Perhaps she asked too many questions.

Jack smiled. "You sure are curious about him. Why do you want...You're sweet on him, aren't you?"

Corrine blushed. "Jack Farley! How dare you?"

Jack threw back his head, laughed, and slapped his bear-bitten leg. Suddenly, his laughing turned to, "OW, that hurt!" as he grabbed his leg and winched in pain.

Corrine, taken by surprise, stared at Jack with her mouth open. Jack looked back to her, and laughed again.

After getting his laughing under control, he rubbed his sore leg. "I'm sorry, I shouldn't have done that. But it sure was funny seeing the look on your face."

Corrine smiled at her old friend. "Well, you're probably right..." then the smile disappeared, "but that's not all there is to it. You know my mother died when I was ten winters old. We talked about that.

"What I didn't tell you was the terrible arguments my parents had late at night, and how, after mother died, Black Wolf, mother's father, was very angry with Father, and how we had to leave Fort Yukon the next day.

"Father treats me like he treated mother. And with all those bad men he suddenly surrounds himself with, I don't feel safe. I've got to get away. I think this Dalton fellow can help. Besides," she said with a half-smile, "I think he fancies me, as well."

Jack's eyes narrowed as he looked directly into hers.

"Corrine, I'm truly sorry to hear all that. Surely, I am. But you got to remember, Dalton's got a stern-wheeler full of trouble coming from your father. You and I both know that. But if he does lend you a hand, don't take that as an invitation into his life, young'un. I have a feelin' he don't want to be harnessed. Expect to get your heart broke."

"Maybe." She said with a smile. "But then maybe that's just what he's looking for and doesn't know it. Can you tell me where he is?"

Jack looked her in the eyes, frowned for a second, and then a thin smile crossed his face. "You'll likely find him down at the dog livery."

* * *

Corrine found Dalton in the back of the livery barn just as Jack had expected.

He sat on a stump, busily replacing the worn out babiche, or thin strips of rawhide, that bound together the ten-foot freight sled.

Steam curled from a pot of water on the wood stove. The pot held more strips of babiche.

As she approached, Corrine noticed the dog she'd seen earlier that day at the Amanita lying by Dalton's side. It growled low.

Dalton cast a sideways glance at her, said something to the dog, and continued to concentrate on what he was doing.

"May I join you?"

"It's a free country." Dalton didn't look at her.

Corrine found an old wooden chair nearby, brought it over, and sat down. She thought a bit, not sure how to open the conversation.

This is crazy. I can't ask him for help. But for some reason, I trust him. Maybe he will take pity on me. She decided to introduce herself, see where it goes. "I'm Corrine Batiste."

"Jon Batiste's daughter. Kinda figured that." Dalton cut the tag-end off a piece of babiche. He nodded toward the door. "Are they waitin' outside for me?"

"Who?"

Dalton fished out another long piece of babiche from the steaming pot, pulled it through his thumb and forefinger, squeezing out the extra moisture.

"Your father and his scoundrels," Dalton wove the babiche through a hole in one of the stanchions and an eye-hook in the runner, securing the stanchion in place.

"No! Heavens no," she said with surprise. *He doesn't trust anyone. He doesn't trust me. But then, why should he?*

"Your father send you here to talk me out of something, or maybe an apology? Cause you're not going to get it."

"No...no, quite the opposite," she said. *I need to get his mind thinking in another direction. Put him more at ease, quit being suspicious of me.* "Your dog seems to be doing well. Not a life-threatening wound, I hope."

Dalton worked on lashing the stanchion down. "My dog's doing fine. Her name is Bandit."

"Because of the black mask?"

Corrine noticed a slight smile cross his face.

"Yes, because of the black mask. How'd you find me anyway?" He looked up at her.

"Jack told me."

"You know Jack?"

Corrine nodded her head, "Yes. He's like a grandfather to me. And, thank you, for what you did for him."

Dalton shrugged his shoulders, looked back down at his work, and tied off the tag-ends of the babiche.

"I'm sure he would have done the same for me." Dalton looked at her. "Now, what are you really here for? I know it's not for polite conversation."

There it was. The moment she was dreading. She began to doubt herself. *What right do I have to ask him for help? He doesn't know me.* She swallowed hard, holding back tears, looked down, shuffled her feet.

"I...don't know where to start." Her voice was barely above a whisper.

"It's usually best to start at the beginning."

She watched him dry his hands on an old towel, and then lay it over the top rail of the sled.

"You know, or at least have a sense, of what my father is like. I need to get out of there, out from under his control." A tear welled up and rolled down her cheek as she thought about her mother. "I can't prove it, but I believe he killed my mother, and, between him and those, scoundrels, as you called them, I'm afraid for my own life."

Dalton looked at her for a moment, his eyes narrowed slightly.

"One thing's for sure, that's no place for a lady. Why don't you just leave?"

Corrine looked away as she wiped her tears. "I have no place to go...no family. My grandfather, *Zhoh Zhraii*, or, Black Wolf in your language, was the last of my mother's people. He died two winters ago." She looked into Dalton's eyes. "Besides, he would find me."

"So, why are you telling me all this?"

Corrine lowered her gaze and recalled the incident at the Amanita.

"When our eyes met this morning, I knew you were someone I could trust." Looking back up at Dalton, she continued, "When

Father told me to go back in the kitchen, I watched you. I know you are a good man."

Dalton crossed his chest with one arm and rested the elbow of the other on the wrist. He rubbed his forehead with his free hand for a while. Corrine wondered if he had a headache.

Dalton uncrossed his arms.

"No...no I'm not getting involved in your family affairs. And I'm sorry, but the last thing I need in my life is a woman! So... no."

CHAPTER 11

The next morning, Dalton left the Nordale Hotel and decided to eat breakfast at another cafe to avoid seeing Citalli. As he sat down at the table, he noticed the man whom he'd seen leaning against the building the day before walk in and take a seat by the front window.

Dalton made eye contact with him, but the man looked away. Dalton thought a bit and then smiled to himself.

His next stop was the hospital and Jack. As he and Bandit walked down First Avenue, he noticed the air was calm. He watched big flakes of snow swirl straight down out of a dull gray sky. It looked to be the beginning of the first big snow of winter. Snow had already piled up a good four inches on the power lines.

Dalton entered Jack's room and shook the snow from his parka before he removed it. He hung it on a coat hook. Dalton observed Jack.

"You're looking good. Color's coming back in your cheeks, I see. The ladies must be treating you well."

Jack frowned at Dalton. "No, they're not. You know they *still* won't let me have a Barthel's beer? And they make me get up and walk the hallway. Says it's good for me. They just like torturing an old man, is all."

Dalton smiled, shook his head, and took a seat in the chair by the bed. "Well, I'm sure they know what's best. You need to exercise that leg and get the soreness out. Get some fresh blood flowin' in that leg."

"Well, maybe. But a fella doesn't have to like it." He looked away.

"No you don't have to like it, but you better do what they tell you to do if you want to get over this. I'm serious.

"I didn't come here to argue with you, but to tell ya what I'm fixin' to do. I've had a tail from Batiste following me around yesterday evening and this morning. By now, he knows where I'm staying, where the dogs are boarded, and where you're at." Dalton shifted in his seat.

"I've been doin' some thinkin' and I think he's going to try to make his move to the Salcha while I'm here in town. It's going to take some time for him to gear up. So... I'm heading over to the marshal's office and talk to my old friend, Dreibelbis, and let him know what's going on. Then, I'm leaving as soon as I pack up. I want to be on familiar ground when the time comes."

It took a minute for Yukon Jack to respond.

"You leaving me behind too? I thought we was partners."

Dalton felt a pang of regret. But what else could he do? *I can't play nurse-maid and protect my trapping grounds at the same time,* he thought.

"I'm concerned about your condition, is all. It's going to be rough out there, and you're in no condition to leave."

Yukon Jack took a deep breath and clenched his jaws.

"Young-un. I got panther blood runnin' through my veins. I just killed a griz with a knife. And I've spent more winters under the northern lights than you have. I *think* I can take care of myself."

"You were just complaining about being tortured by the nurses!"

"Aw, I was just jawin'. I like to give 'em a hard time."

He sure is a tough old bull, Dalton thought. "Look. I gotta go *now*. If you feel up to it, in a few days, when the doctor releases you, head on out to the Salcha. But go the back way in."

Jack smiled. "Now you're talkin'." The smile disappeared as Jack looked seriously at Dalton. "There's a back way in?"

"Yep. Make your way to Ollie Olson's place on the South Fork of the Chena. He's worth his salt. Tell him everything that's happened and ask him to give you directions to my upper line cabin on Gold Creek—where it enters the North Fork of the Salcha. Tell him I could sure use his help too, if he can spare it. If I'm not at the cabin, make yourself comfortable. I'll be along sometime."

"Alright. Dalton?"

"Now what?"

"Did you talk to Corrine?"

"Yes."

"You gonna help her?"

"Jack, I don't have time for a woman in my life. You know that. She'll be alright. Besides, I got too much on my plate as it is."

"No, she won't be alright, and yeah, you do have a lot on your plate, but you need to skootch some things around and make room for this one. That's all I'm sayin'." Jack waved his hand as a king dismisses his subject, urging Dalton to the door.

***

It snowed heavily on the well-packed

Valdez Trail, and even though he had a heavy load of supplies, Dalton made good time.

Bandit seemed to have no problems with her shoulder, other than a little stiffness, which she soon worked out. They settled into a ground-eating pace and the monotony of good, fast, trail travel.

Dalton took out his Copenhagen, took a dip, then replaced it in the inside pocket of his parka and reminisced about the last couple of days.

He could understand why Batiste would be interested in the furs of the Salcha Valley. Some of the best furs came from Dalton's trapline. He had spent years farming them, taking only the excess, ensuring breeding stock for the future. He'd tried to keep the wolves in check because even they had their place, he believed. Most people thought otherwise. That wolves should be eradicated. But Dalton believed God had a reason for creating them, as well.

It's a fact the wolves often seemed to kill much more than they needed. Sometimes killing a dozen or more healthy adults and calves out of a herd of caribou, then leaving them lay, leaving a wake of destruction behind. Not unlike Jon Batiste.

Dalton's jaws tightened. *Like he said, he'll 'do anything he can to get his share of the wealth. It'll take too long to set all those traps, though. Too much weight, not enough men. How could somebody come in and clean out most of the fur in a short amount of time?* he wondered.

A thought struck him like a mild, electric shock. Even though there were no laws against it, the thought repulsed him. *Poison! He's going to use strychnine! It'll be much easier to pack in. That son-of-a-gun is going to end up killing everything from whiskey jacks to wolves.*

"Whoa!" Dalton called out to his team as he stood on the break.

They came to a stop and Dalton stomped the snow hook into the hard-packed trail snow. He shook the accumulated snow from the fur ruff around his parka hood, then threw the hood back as he walked up to the team.

He petted each one, checking to make sure they were in good spirits and not sulking—an indication something might be wrong.

After about a fifteen-minute break, the dogs got antsy, ready to go again. Dalton pulled the snow hook and gave the command "Hike!"

The team settled into a graceful lope and Corrine suddenly flashed through his brain.

The memory of her had often crossed his mind since seeing her in the Amanita, but he had successfully fought it down —each time taking longer than the last. Unbeknownst to her, she had gripped his heart like a number four Newhouse wolf trap and held on hard.

Come on you fool! She's no different than the rest. She just wants to use you. She proved that at the dog livery when she wanted you to help her get away from her father.

Somehow, he didn't quite believe it. There had to be more to it than that. He felt ashamed he'd turned her down.

What if she's right? What if Batiste is capable of murdering his own daughter?

It's rumored he murdered at least one Indian, if not more in his lust for money. And the rest of those men... The thought made him shudder.

What if I just signed her death warrant by refusing my help? I could never live with myself. But what could I do? I couldn't buy her passage on the riverboats. The last one left over a week ago. Then, he chastised himself. *You're such a cad. You idiot!*

But what could he have done? *Bring her out here with me?* Dalton smiled at the thought. *That would really chap Batiste's hide.*

Visibility was less than a hundred yards now because of the heavy snowfall, and a good foot of new snow had built up on the trail. He heard the dogs barking well before Munson's Roadhouse came into view. Jimmy met them at the dog barn and held the door open while Dalton drove the team inside.

Dalton rested the dogs and checked the leather moccasins he'd put on Chinook's feet to protect her tender pads. They were in good shape and her pads seemed to be healing nicely. He was impressed with Ed's home-made liniment, and he'd told him so when he checked the dogs over earlier that morning.

While checking the load, the thought crossed his mind to ask Munson for back up, if and when the time came. Then, he was embarrassed he even thought of it. Of course, he couldn't. What was he thinking? Munson had a wife and a business to think about.

Stepping inside the roadhouse, the aroma of coffee, freshly baked sourdough bread, and beans aroused his nostrils.

"Mrs. Munson, I'd be eternally grateful for some of what you got cooking in there," Dalton said, as he hung his parka on the nail by the door.

"Yeah, sit yourself down and I'll get ya some." Mrs. Munson got up from the table.

Dalton took a few steps toward the long wooden table and glanced at Mr. Munson. Munson opened his mouth to say something to Dalton but got cut off by the Missus.

"Headin' back out to the bush?"

Dalton glanced at her, then back at the table as he sat down. "Yes, ma'am. Gotta start getting the traps ready."

He looked back at Mr. Munson, who again opened his mouth to talk and again got cut off by the Missus.

"How's Jack doing? Better?" She placed a cup in front of Dalton.

Dalton watched with amusement as Mr. Munson shook his head and began to study the inside of his coffee cup.

Dalton smiled, looked back at his own cup, and wrapped both hands around it, enjoying the warmth.

"Yes, much better. The doctor's got him up walking around and Jack's itchin' to get out of there. I think Doc wants to keep him there for a while, though."

Mrs. Munson snorted as she walked back to the kitchen, "Betcha that old coot walks out on his own in a day or two, whether the doctor wants him to or not."

Dalton studied the contents of his cup, also.

"You're probably right Mrs. Munson." Looking over at Mr. Munson, Dalton watched him look up to check on the Missus. She was busy plating up Dalton's food.

Munson looked at Dalton and said with a hushed tone, "So how'd it go with Batiste?"

"Not good. He refused to back down. There was a scuffle. And Bandit got cut."

"Bad?"

"No. She's okay."

A moment of silence filled the space between them.

"You know, Dalton, in my younger days, I'd be right there by your side."

Dalton looked over at Munson and saw the embarrassment in his face.

"No. No, don't worry about it. I understand completely. You have a wife and a business to run. Besides, this is my fight. Not anyone else's."

Munson looked back at his coffee. "I don't envy you at all."

During supper, Dalton wrote out a telegram and gave it to Jimmy along with another silver dollar, and told him to get it to the telegraph office as soon as possible.

Dalton washed the last of his supper down with another cup of coffee. He gathered up his parka and headed to the dog barn.

From here on, the snow would be deeper to his line cabin on Ninetyeight Creek, but at least it would have a bottom to it from his earlier run a couple of days ago, with Jack. From there to his main cabin on No Grub Creek he'd be breaking trail all the way.

CHAPTER 12

The steel gray clouded sky grew dim, and slushy ice floated downstream as they crossed the river. By the time Dalton changed his socks and mukluks, the sun had set and the last mile of trail to the Ninetyeight Creek cabin was made in the dark. He trusted Bandit to keep the trail and guide them home. All he had to worry about was keeping the sled upright and protecting his face from low hanging, snow-laden willow and alder branches.

Soon, he was able to make out the dark outline of the cabin walls as they pulled into the yard. Dalton unhitched the dogs, starting with the wheel dogs and worked forward, depending on Bandit to keep the tug line taut and the other dogs in line until their turn came. He checked each dog carefully for possible injuries and praised them for a job well done. Bandit was turned loose to run freely.

An unwritten code of the north is preference for the dogs. A man was lower than the lowest if he did not take care of them properly. They're your means of transportation. They gave you their all. They're your companions. They are family. You are the leader of the pack, and you take care of them appropriately.

Tonight, the dogs would have a hearty meal.

Dalton started a fire under a section of a steel drum he used as a cauldron and packed it with snow to melt. To this, he added rice, tallow, and chopped dried fish. He brought it up to a simmer. The hungry dogs became restless, anticipating warm food. While that was cooking, only then did he go inside the cabin to start the fire in the stove.

When he returned, the porridge had thickened. Dalton ladled it up equally and fed his team, starting with Bandit. The next two hours he spent fixing his own supper, cleaning up, unpacking, and storing some of the supplies in the cache. The rest would be distributed between the other two cabins.

Dalton sat on his bunk, mentally going through the checklist of things done. Satisfied, he yawned. It had been a long sixteen-hour day, and tomorrow was going to be rough.

Sleep was slow in coming as he thought about the trail ahead.

He had twenty miles, or so, of trail to break. The snowshoes weighed about five pounds each, and the added weight of snow buildup on the toes would add a couple more.

He'd not used snowshoes since last winter, and he wasn't used to it. He knew from experience he would be lame by the time they got to No Grub. It would take a day or two to heal completely. The Canadian Voyageurs used to call it *Mal de Raquette*, or snowshoe sickness.

Nevertheless, Dalton felt a sense of urgency —the need to push on. He was going to have to live with it until he reached the high country. He felt more at ease there.

* * *

His internal alarm clock woke him well before sun-up. It was still snowing, though lightly, as he stepped outside and pulled his martin-skin hat over his ears. Clouds of frozen water vapor from his breath frosted his beard and the fur around his hat before it drifted away in the still air.

As is often the case in the interior, when the snow clouds leave and it clears up, the bottom drops out of the thermometer. Dalton knew that when the day was done, it would probably hit twenty below. Perfect working weather for him and the dogs.

He was glad he had dressed in layers. His concern was not for the cold, but for overheating and breaking a sweat while breaking trail. If he got sweaty, the trapped moisture would freeze when he took a rest, possibly creating hypothermic conditions. Instead, he would peel off enough layers until he felt cool while working so he would not sweat. This would allow what moisture he created to escape. He could always replace the layers as needed when he took a break.

Dalton stashed the runner sled on the roof of the cabin and pulled down the toboggan sled. It would provide more flotation on the two-and-a-half feet of snow that had fallen, instead of sinking and becoming a plow, as the basket sled would do.

Laying out a large oilcloth to cover the basket of the sled, with the excess hanging over the top rails, handlebar, and brush bow, Dalton loaded the supplies, making sure to place the heaviest weight in the back. He folded over the excess tarp, enveloping the load and lashed down, keeping the contents dry. The important items which would be needed throughout the day were strategically placed for handy access. The Winchester in the scabbard lashed on the inside of the sled, butt facing the driver, ax, in its own scabbard, snowshoes lashed to the top of the load, and food in a pouch slung under the handlebar, next to the snow-hook holster.

Just as the sun peeked over the horizon behind the thinning clouds, Dalton pulled the snow hook and gave the command. It was nearly eight o'clock. At the river crossing, Dalton gave Bandit the command of "Haw!" She dutifully turned the team left and headed upstream, instead of crossing the river.

Fifteen yards later, Dalton confirmed he would have to break trail all the way to No Grub Creek. After calling the team to a halt, he removed his mittens and let them hang from the cord that ran from one mitten to the other through the arms of his parka. He untied the snowshoes from the sled and buckled the bindings to his feet. He removed his parka and lashed it on top of the load.

Squatting down in front of Bandit, he took her big head in his hands. "Stay behind me girl. You know what to do, keep those guys in line." He ruffled up the fur on both sides of her neck as she licked his face. He gave her a hug, stood, then turned upstream and trudged through the snow, breaking trail. About thirty feet in front of the dogs, he gave Bandit the command of "Come easy."

* * *

Late that night at his main cabin on No Grub Creek, Dalton's knees ached and his calf and thigh muscles burned and cramped as he fed the dogs. He stumbled through the door of his cabin and plopped down on the bunk. Ten miles out, he wasn't quite sure he would make it. Thankfully, the snow hadn't fallen quite so deep in the upper part of the valley, and Dalton was able to ride the last five miles.

He spent the rest of the night wrapping his abused legs in steaming hot towels, then rubbing them down with icy snow. Sleep escaped him as overtaxed leg muscle spasms jerked him awake. By morning, he could walk tolerably well.

He thought about spending a day there to heal up some more and get some much-needed rest for him and the dogs. But a nagging sense of urgency convinced him he needed to move on to the high country.

Besides, it was beginning to snow again.

CHAPTER 13

Frank Ward knew Jon Batiste was in a surly mood. Gee pole Larson, the tail Batiste had put on Dalton, reported there was talk going around town how Dalton had walked right into Batiste's saloon and told him in no uncertain terms to stay out of the Salcha. But what put the rest of the men a little on edge was finding out that Yukon Jack was indeed alive and in the hospital. The whispered talk going around town the Syndicate had something to do with it, didn't help matters much.

Ward wondered aloud that Dalton might have started the gossip.

Batiste threw a scowling look at Ward.

"What difference does it make? It's out there and there's nothing we can do about it. It's not going to affect my plans one way or the other. Besides, if it was Dalton or those drunk miners who were in here, they can't prove a thing. *Non*, I think it was Jack. And as long as he's in the hospital, there is really nothing we can do to shut him up. But when he gets out, he just might disappear under the Chena River ice."

Batiste leaned back in his chair and locked his fingers across his fat belly, apparently in deep thought. Then, squinting his eyes, he looked at each man standing around the table. The last person he looked at was Ward.

"Ward."

Ward's muscles suddenly tensed up like a rabbit sensing danger but not knowing from where it might come.

He knew he had lost some respect from the rest of the gang when Dalton notched his ear a couple of days ago. The gang only did what he told them to do because they knew he was still Batiste's ramrod. Ward wondered how long it would be before someone began to challenge him.

"Ya, boss?"

"You've been with me for a couple of years now, and I respect your judgment."

Ward relaxed a little, enjoying the compliment, but still wary.

"You trust these men?" Batiste stared directly in Ward's eyes.

Ward glance around and noticed they all held their eyes on him. He looked back at Batiste.

"Not any further than I could throw them. I've known most of these men since the Klondike. They're devious and cunning, which makes them good fightin' men. That's why I recommended them to ya. Now if you're askin' if they're loyal? Yes. As long as they get a paycheck."

Batiste stared at Ward for a brief moment. Then a smile slowly appeared.

"*Oui*, they'll get a paycheck, all right. If this goes according to plan, we'll have a mighty heavy poke come breakup. No? I've got a market lined up in Seattle that's paying top dollar for all the furs I can ship to him.

"Only problem is, I've spent a small fortune in strychnine and other gear to outfit these men and I don't want any of them getting any fool notions in their heads."

Ward felt a smile cross his face while thinking he had just dodged a bullet.

"Like I said boss, they're loyal. Give 'em a good grubstake and a promise of adventure and they're happy."

Batiste unlaced his fingers from across his belly, leaned toward Ward.

"All right. I'm counting on your judgment. But if anyone screws up, I'll notch your other ear. You understand?"

Ward involuntarily reached up to rub the sore ear Dalton had notched. He felt a wave of embarrassment wash over him, then anger as he relived the events and heard the snickers from the rest of the gang.

Ward looked down at the table. "I understand, Boss."

Batiste leaned back in his chair. "*Bon*! Now, if you've got everything packed and ready to go, it's time to move."

* * *

Frank Ward replayed that conversation in his mind later that afternoon when they spotted the cabin on Ninetyeight Creek.

It'd been easy to find. All they had to do was follow Dalton's sled trail. They tied up the five teams, heavily loaded with supplies about a hundred yards from the cabin, and crept close to observe the cabin for signs of activity.

No smoke rose from the chimney and no dogs were in the dog yard—a good sign no one was there.

After bringing the teams on up to the cabin, Ward instructed the four men to start feeding the dogs. Ward would check things out.

First was the cache, hoping to find anything of value. Furs, firearms, or food.

No furs were found, and no firearms. He did find a couple of boxes of 30-30 ammunition which he stashed in his parka pocket

119

for his own use, and plenty of meat, beans, bacon, flour, and other staples.

The cabin was next. Stepping inside with his gear, Ward paused a bit, letting his eyes adjust to the dark interior.

It was a Spartan affair, as most trappers' cabins are. Built small, less space to heat, but skookum, well-made with tight-fitting notches that needed little, if any chinking. An old parka hung on a nail driven into one of the logs by the door. A table, a couple of chairs, counter tops, and shelves, all made from hand-sawed lumber, lined the walls. Pots and pans hung on nails behind the flat-topped wood stove.

He noticed a bunk bed against the far wall, made of slender spruce poles, covered in caribou hides for a mattress. Ward walked to it and laid down his bedroll.

That'll be mine, he mused. *The others will just have to sleep on the floor.*

Ward's attention returned to the stove. Taking a couple of steps to the stove, he unlatched and swung open the little door and stuck his hand inside. A little bit of heat radiated up from the ashes. After opening the damper, his breath caressed the ashes. Ward smiled as a couple of small embers began to glow.

We're not too far behind you, Dalton.

Soon, he had a fire going in the stove. Just

as he finished putting a couple of good-sized chunks of wood on the blaze and closed the stove's door, the other four men entered the cabin carrying their bedrolls.

Ward decided it was a good time to assert his authority.

"The bunks mine." He stood and turned to face the men. "You boys can throw some robes on the floor and sack out there."

The other men cast sideways glances at each other with looks of disgust on their faces. Ward paid them no attention.

Hank was the first to speak up. "Why do *you* get the bunk?"

Ward gritted his teeth. He didn't like Hank much. He was a surly sort of fella who didn't like authority. It irritated Ward every time Hank questioned him or offered unwanted advice. However, if anyone knew the bush, it was Hank.

Ward turned his head and looked Hank in the eye. Then, putting as much edge to his voice as he could, said, "Cause I'm running this outfit and I said so."

Ward looked at each of the others in turn. "Any of you other boys got a problem with that?"

The others evidently decided they did not have a problem with that and agreed that sleeping on the robes of caribou skins was good for them. Ward watched as Hank looked at the others, shook his head, and sat down at the table.

While the others were laying out their bedrolls, Ward sat on the bunk.

"I've decided the best way to take over Dalton's trapline is simply to occupy his cabins. I figure there's got to be the main cabin somewhere up the valley. If we have two men on each cabin watching the trail, we could restrict him to the upper Salcha until reinforcements arrive.

"Smith, I want you and Gee pole Larson to stay here and watch this place. The three of us will head upriver in the morning and find the other cabin. Dalton was kind enough to break trail for us, and by tomorrow, it should have a good bottom to it. As soon as we get established, I'll send for reinforcements."

"Well, if I was you, I'd send for 'em now. Dalton is one tough son-of-a-wolf," Hank half muttered under his breath.

Ward's anger grew and his light complexion showed the red in his face as he struggled to contain it.

"Well, you ain't me so don't worry about it. Your job is to do what I tell ya. You, me, and the Swede will be leaving in the morning."

"What do you want us to do while you're gone?" Gee pole Larson asked.

"Start catchin' fur. There's got to be a couple of traplines leading off from this place, and like most trappers, he probably leaves his traps hangin' in the trees from one year to the next. Find 'em and use 'em.

"You also have three bottles of strychnine in the sled bag. You know how to use that. Kill a moose and put out poison baits up and down the river. "

You also have your rifles. If you can't trap it or poison it, shoot it. The boss wants to clean the fur out of this valley, and we're gonna do it."

CHAPTER 14

Dalton sat cross-legged on the hillside with Bandit at his side. They were behind his upper line cabin on Gold Creek, just upstream from where it emptied into the North Fork of the Salcha.

There had been less snow in the upper Salcha, so he didn't have to break trail with the snowshoes like the day before, for which he was thankful. The day had dawned bitter cold once again.

Movement caught Dalton's eye as he watched his back-trail down the North Fork Valley. Pulling the binoculars from his parka pocket, he placed his elbows on his knees to steady his hands.

Moving the eyepiece into focus, he found what had caught his attention. A pack of six wolves trotted single file down the sled trail, appearing and then disappearing like ghosts in the brush, headed toward the Salcha Valley.

Dalton lowered the binoculars, stared hard at the line of moving dots, and then held his breath so he wouldn't fog the lenses as he brought the binoculars back up to his eyes. He grinned and gave out a little grunt as he recognized the lead wolf. A big black alpha male with a tinge of gray on his hips and muzzle.

"I'll be dadgummed. That's your papa down there, Bandit." Dalton kept his eyes on the pack. The sight pleased him, as he'd not seen the big male in over a year.

Bandit stuck her muzzle under Dalton's armpit and raised her head so he'd pet her. This disrupted his vision. He laughed at her and scratched behind her ears. He brought the binoculars back up to his eyes just in time to watch the wolves disappear around the bend toward the mouth of the North Fork.

They both sat there for a few moments, and then it struck him. *Black Wolf. Wasn't that what Corrine said her grandfather's name was?* A wave of guilt washed over him as he remembered how she had come to him for help. He'd turned her down. He'd violated his own beliefs. In this harsh environment, you're supposed to help each other out.

You never know when it might be your turn. Just like Jack. Well, maybe the telegram I sent him will help... if it's not too late.

Another thought crossed his mind.

Has Batiste made his move? I wouldn't be surprised if they were somewhere on the Salcha right now. If they find the main cabin

*—and it wouldn't be hard to do—I'd have a
tough time flushing them out.*

He decided to head back to the main cabin
in the dark of the night to find out.

* * *

When Dalton stepped out of the cabin later
that evening, he noticed something downriver
attracted the dogs' attention. Jumping up on
their houses with ears erect, they all stared
into the gathering dark. Tension filled the
air. Then, barely perceptible in the intense
cold, he heard it. The low melodious howls
of wolves rejoicing over a kill, as if offering
up thanks.

The howls abruptly stopped. A minute later,
one lone baritone voice continued. It didn't
sound right—almost mournful. A feeling of
concern crept over Dalton and slid down his
back like an icy hand. Something wasn't right,
but just what it was, he didn't know.

Dalton turned the dogs loose to play a
little and laid out the tug line and harnesses.
Starting with Bandit, he called each one by
name, then harnessed and clipped each into
the tug line in their turn.

He knew reading the trail through the dark
timber would be a little tricky, but out in the
flats the moon's reflection off the snow—
three days past full—and the northern lights,

if there were any, would brighten things up a bit. Besides, he trusted Bandit to find the trail.

As he loaded the sled, he mentally checked off the items he wanted. It would be a fast trip with a light load. His possibles bag contained a survival kit, axe, extra clothes, and his caribou-hide sleeping bag was all he took. The 30-30, of course, he stowed in its scabbard.

Dalton pulled the snow hook, gave the command, and soon they reached the mouth of the North Fork.

The wind picked up in the valley, which was unusual for this time of year, and swirling clouds of miniature ice crystals obliterated all traces of his trail. They stung like pinpricks on his exposed cheeks.

Standing on the brake, Dalton slowed the dogs to a halt and pulled the wolverine ruff on his parka hood a little closer around his face for protection. The light levels were lower, but still light enough to make out objects as far as the swirling snow would allow.

The next obstacle was crossing the main channel. Dalton studied the river and gave it some thought.

When he crossed two days prior, there'd been shelf ice to contend with. It'd been the same story as before. Find a shallow spot, get wet while crossing, build a fire, change out socks and foot gear while the dogs chewed the ice balls from between their toes, and move on.

Dalton knew building a fire in this wind was out of the question. There had been slush ice and chunks floating downriver before. With the continued cold, those miniature icebergs had grown bigger and congealed together with the shelf ice. The shallow places were no longer safe to cross because the rushing water underneath kept the ice thin.

Dalton realized he'd forgotten to bring extra foot gear. The safest place to cross would be the deeper, slower pools where the ice was somewhat thicker. But was it thick enough after three days of twenty below? That was the question.

This time, Dalton didn't use the snow hook to anchor the sled to the trail. Instead, he took Bandit's head in his hands and, looking her in the eyes, gave her the command to 'Stay!'

He took the axe out of the sled, cut a long, slender pole, and walked downstream to the edge of the river, where he found a deeper pool of water. Holding the pole at the balance point under his left arm—just in case he went through—Dalton swung the axe with his right arm at arm's length in front of himself onto the ice. If it went through, the ice was too thin.

It stopped with a satisfying *thunk*. Taking another step forward, he repeated the process. Dalton made it all the way across, scrambled up the bank, then called the team to follow. Through the blowing snow, he watched them approach. Bandit pulled low, sniffing out her master's scent and checking the ice.

With the team safely on the other side, Dalton replaced the axe and stuffed the pole in the sled, thinking he might need it again. The rest of the trail to the next river crossing should be fairly easy.

The wind died down somewhat with occasional gusts, and the reflected moonlight brightened as they made their way downstream. The blowing snow had completely obliterated the trail, but Bandit's unerring judgment kept the sled on track.

About two-and-a-half miles later, as they came off a side-hill trail onto the flats, Bandit slowed the team and looked back at her master. Dalton could tell she was concerned about something but wasn't sure what. After breaking the team to a stop, he stomped the snow hook into the trail.

"What's wrong, Bandit?"

She looked at him, then toward the river on their right. Dalton scanned the flats and noticed what looked to be a tuft of hair sticking up from a snowdrift.

Pulling his rifle, he stepped off the runners and into knee-deep snow and waded his way to the drift. Just before he reached it, he realized it was moose hair.

Must be the wolf kill. Okay. No big deal. I expected that. Hmm. There doesn't seem to be much of it, for an animal the size of a moose.

As Dalton turned to walk back to the sled, he stumbled over something buried in the snow. Looking down to see what he had stumbled over, he noticed fur sticking up from the disturbed snow.

Dalton kicked the snow away and uncovered...a dead wolf.

Dalton checked the wolf over, looking for signs of injury. Perhaps the others from the pack had killed it. But no, the fur was in good shape, not torn up.

So, how did it die?

Dalton looked back at the moose, thought a bit, and then walked up to it. He kicked the snow away to uncover as much of the animal as he could.

The only thing he found was a chunk of moose shoulder, frozen solid, with gnaw marks from the wolves. One side left untouched by the wolves, he found the marks of an axe, left behind by whoever chopped the piece of meat from the frozen carcass.

Bait. Just as I thought. They're using poison bait.

Dalton's jaw muscles tightened and the realization made him sick. Dalton shook his head and turned toward the sled. Glancing down at the dead wolf, he wondered about the big black. Had he survived? Perhaps the one, lone, lonely howl he had heard was his. Dalton hoped so.

Man, I got to get these scum-bags outta here. They're gonna kill everything.

Back on the trail, it wasn't long before Dalton caught a glimpse of his cabin through the dark gusting swirls of snow, across the river on No Grub Creek. Once or twice he thought he caught the scent of wood smoke in the swirling eddies, but wasn't sure.

To heck with it! Dalton stepped off the runners. *I gotta get closer.*

He tied the sled to a clump of willows, took a dip of Copenhagen, reached for his Winchester, jacked a round in the chamber, and eased the hammer down.

Pulling the pole from the sled, he waded through the knee-deep snow to Bandit, and then leaned the pole against a willow.

Taking her big head in his hand, he said, "Bandit, you're going to have to sing for me girl." She licked him on the face. "Sing for me. Aoooohhh. You can do it."

And then, she did. A deep wolf howl erupted from her throat as she laid back her ears and pointed her nose to the sky.

The other wolf dogs in the team joined in and a chorus of howls filled the night.

No sooner had he hushed his dogs, he had his answer. At his cabin off in the distance, huskies answered back.

Yep, someone's at the cabin alright. But how many?

Dalton patted Bandit's head. "Bandit, stay. I'll be back."

Dalton pushed his way through the snow to the river's edge, rifle in one hand and pole in the other. Holding the pole like a spear, he jabbed the end into the ice in front of him as he eased along. Half-way across, he heard an ominous *CRACK* underfoot and quickly fell backward to spread out his weight.

Rolling over onto his hands and knees, he crawled back a few feet to stronger ice and stood up.

Whew, that was close, he thought. Checking his weapon, he found that snow had gotten into his gun barrel.

I can't worry about that now. Thankfully, the gun is as cold as the snow, so it won't melt and stick to the metal.

Dalton worked his way a few feet upstream and found stronger ice. He made it across, then made his way toward the cabin—close enough to see wisps of smoke rising from the chimney.

Plucking a small twig from a willow, he cleaned the snow out of the end of the barrel.

A quietness took over the land as large snow-flakes fell from the sky.

They're well-fortified behind those thick logs. The only way to get 'em out is to smoke 'em out.

All he had to do was sneak up on the roof and cover the stovepipe with his parka. Then, as they came out, he'd have the advantage of elevation, and he could easily drive them off.

Dalton cocked the hammer of his Winchester and made his way across the clearing in front of the cabin.

About half-way across, he heard the creak of the cabin door. Dalton looked up and found himself staring into the eyes of the man they called Hank.

Hank cursed and dove for the door. Dalton, caught in the open, turned and headed back to the river. He felt a bullet tug at his parka and, at the same time, heard the report of a rifle.

He felt the sting of hot lead under his left arm and he knew he'd been hit. The force of the bullet was enough to spin him around. He fell to the snow on his back.

Dalton watched as Ward and the Swede piled out of the cabin, back-lit by the light spilling from inside.

What Dalton focused on most, though, was the grin on Hank's face as he charged toward Dalton.

In the moment it takes lightning to reach the earth, Dalton thought, *So, this is how it ends. All I have worked for will go to them. NO! Fight, you fool.*

Still on his back in the snow, Dalton swung the Winchester, leveled it at Hank, and, without aiming, pulled the trigger— all in one fluid motion.

His instincts were true.

Hank abruptly stopped, with a look of shocked surprise on his face. Hank looked down.

Dalton followed his gaze and saw a dark red splotch growing on Hank's shirt. Hank touched it, then rubbed the dark red sticky liquid between his fingers.

Grinning at Dalton, Hank fell to his knees and then face-forward into the snow.

Dalton watched Ward and the Swede shove each other out of the way, trying to get back into the cabin.

Dalton struggled to his feet. He needed to return to his dogs.

The burning sensation grew worse, and the feeling of wetness on his left side almost made him retch as he stumbled through the snow toward the sled.

He wondered if Ward and the Swede would come back out with guns blazing to finish the job.

He got his answer as hot lead whined and ricochet through the willows, like angry yellow jackets.

CHAPTER 15

It was Saturday evening. Corrine was in the kitchen of the Amanita, preparing meals for the men and the patrons when she heard someone come crashing through the back door.

She was about to walk through the kitchen door into the bar to see what the commotion was about, when she overheard the Swede whispering about someone getting shot. She stopped, just inside the kitchen door and listened.

"*Sacrebleu*, Swede. Start over," her father said.

"Like I was saying, Hank stepped out of the cabin last night to use the outhouse and caught Dalton sneakin' up from the river. He come back in and grabbed his rifle and took a pot shot at 'im. He never was much of a shot. Anyways, the noise woke me and Ward up and we dove out the cabin to see what the commotion was about, and that's when it happened."

"When what happened, Swede?"

A lump arose in Corrine's throat and she bit her upper lip to stifle her fear that Dalton was hurt or, worse yet, dead.

"Dalton kilt Hank."

Relief flooded over her as she realized Dalton must be all right. Then, the Swede continued.

"But Hank got in a good lick afore he died. We found blood where Dalton fell and tracked him to where he had tied up his sled across the river."

"Did ya get him?"

"No. He got away."

"Where's Ward?" Batiste asked.

"He's at the main cabin. He sent me back with Hank's body and to get some help."

"What about the other two?"

"They were at the lower cabin. I sent them to join up with Ward."

"Alright men. Get packed up and be back here in thirty minutes. Swede, grab that dynamite in the back room. We may need it," Batiste ordered.

"But Boss, what about Hank?" the Swede asked.

"What about him?"

"What do you want me to do with him?"

"Anyone see him on your sled?"

"Well no, I don't t'ink so. He's covered with a tarp and I tied the dogs up in the alley." The Swede said.

"*Bon*. Leave him back there. He'll freeze solid if he ain't already, and we'll take care of him later."

Corrine was numb. Fear welled up inside her as tears rolled down her cheeks. The only man she had trusted to help her, the only man she—dare she say it? —loved, was wounded and possibly dying out there all alone, somewhere, in the vast winter wilderness.

Oh, how she longed to be with him now. To hold him. To comfort him. To take care of him.

Had she detected a twinge of guilt in his voice when he refused to help her? She believed she had.

I know he feels the same way about me as I do for him. He just won't admit it. Something deep down inside is holding him back. But, that's okay, she told herself. *Because someday, I know he'll come around.*

None of that mattered. What mattered was going to him. To be there for him.

But how? I have a team of dogs, but I don't know how to get to the Salcha. And if I did, I couldn't possibly beat my father and his men. They will be gone within the hour.

Then she thought of Jack.

That's it! He'll know what to do.

* * *

Corrine shoved the hospital door open and rushed past the nurse at the front desk, headed for Yukon Jack's room.

"Wait a minute. Ma'am? MA'AM, WHERE ARE YOU GOING?" the nurse yelled as Corrine rushed by. "VISITING HOURS ARE OVER! HEY! COME BACK HERE!"

Corrine ignored her and rushed down the hall to Jack's room. She opened the door, glanced back at the nurse, and saw her on the phone, looking sternly at Corrine.

Corrine slipped through the door, and closed it behind her. She made eye contact with Jack.

"I think I've died and the angels are here to get me." Jack grinned.

Corrine crossed the room and sat down at Jack's bed. "Jack, listen to me. They've shot Dalton, and Father and the rest of the syndicate just left to hunt him down. I've got to get to him."

Jack's smile disappeared and a look of concern crossed his face.

"What? How'd he get shot?"

"I was listening from the kitchen door and

I heard the Swede say something about Dalton trying to drive Ward, Hank, and the Swede out of his cabin. Hank caught him in the open and fired first and hit him, but Dalton fired back and killed Hank. And now they're all headed out there to find him. Oh, Jack, what am I gonna do? I need to be with him."

Yukon Jack turned his eyes from her and looked toward the ceiling. He closed his eyes and she saw the muscles in his jaw tighten.

Looking back at her, he said, "We'll just have to go to him, that's all. I got a telegram from him that said for me to bring you with me when I got out of the hospital. This is as good a time as any."

"Dalton said that?" she asked with surprise.

Jack smiled. "Yep."

"He wants me out there with him?"

"Yep."

"But you can't go. You haven't completely healed up yet."

"I've healed enough, young'un. Help me find my clothes." Jack pushed himself up into a sitting position on the edge of the bed.

Corrine moved toward the dresser to find his clothes. The door of the room opened and the front desk nurse walked in.

"Ma'am, I'm going to have to ask you to leave. I've called the doctor and ... Sir?

What are you doing?" The nurse stared at Jack in disbelief.

"I'm fixin' to put my clothes on, and if you don't want to see a hairy, naked sourdough such as myself, you better leave and close the door."

"Oh no, you don't. You better…"

Jack stood up and unbuttoned his robe. The nurse turned red as a highbush cranberry and backed out the door.

Corrine, temporarily forgetting her despair, handed Jack his clothes. "That certainly got rid of her."

Jack laid out his clothes on the bed. "Yeah. I'm sure it's a sight to behold."

Corrine turned her back and looked out the window, as Jack got dressed.

"Jack? How are we going to do it? How are we going to get there before Father? He'll have a head start."

"Dalton told me the other day how to get to his upper cabin the back way. He said to make it to Ollie Olsen's place on the South Fork of the Chena. He could guide us from there.

"Looking back, I have a notion he had an idea something might happen. Anyway, it just so happens that Ollie was in town the other day gettiin' supplies and stopped in to see how I was doin'. Seems as though Dalton told him about me when he was over there a gettin' his dogs to bring me to town.

"He's got a trapline on the South Fork just over the ridge from Dalton's line. It's a somewhat shorter distance to the upper Salcha. Guess we'll have to rent a team of dogs. You can turn around now."

Corrine turned back to face Jack, and gave him a crooked smile.

"Don't worry about that. I've got a team at the dog barn."

Jack looked at her wide-eyed. "You got dogs?"

"Siberian and Eskimo dog crossbreeds."

Jack looked stunned for a minute, and then said, "I didn't know that. Does your father know?"

"Nobody does, except Ed, the proprietor."

"How'd you come by them?" Jack grunted in pain as he pulled one mukluk on.

"I bought 'em from a miner that sold out and headed back to the States. He mushed 'em here from Nome two winters ago."

"Well don't that beat all," Jack reached for the other mukluk.

"Jack?"

"Yes, young'un?"

Corrine hesitated. She decided her next question needed to be asked.

"You think you can handle the trail? I don't want to have to play nursemaid to two men."

Jack grunted as he pulled on the other boot.

"He saved my life, now he needs my help. Ain't nothin' goin' to stop me from gettin' there."

"Alright, then," Corrine said. "I'll call Ed and have him harness up the dogs and drive them here to the hospital. I'll meet you out front when you're ready."

"Oh, by the way," Jack picked up an envelope lying on the bedside table. "Deputy Dreibelbis dropped this off for me to give to Dalton next time I saw him."

"What is it?" she asked.

Jack stuffed the envelope into his shirt pocket. "Don't know. But he wanted me to make sure Dalton got it. Said it was from the Chief Deputy and really important. Remind me to give it to him when we see him. Would ya?"

"Alright." She turned to leave.

Under the watchful glare of the nurse at the reception desk, Corrine hung up the phone after talking to Ed. The front door opened and in walked the doctor, followed by a gust of cold air and swirling snowflakes.

"This is the *lady* I was telling you about, Doctor," the nurse said, with obvious disdain in her voice.

The doctor closed the door and shook the snow from his parka. Yukon Jack limped his way to the receptionist desk. The doctor looked at Corrine then at Jack and back to Corrine.

"Corrine, what's going on?"

Briefly, Corrine explained their situation. "Please, Doc. Let me take him. I need his help."

The doctor looked Jack up and down. "Well... I'm surprised he's made as good of progress as he has. The swelling in his leg has gone down quite a bit, and he can see with both eyes well enough. Besides, he gives my nurses the fits.

"All right. He can go. But I got to warn ya about a couple of things. First, even though I pulled the stitches a couple of days ago, be careful about opening those wounds back up. Second, it's dark out there and you have a long way to travel. There's a storm brewing. It's warming up and already started to snow. It might be another good one, I can feel it in my bones. I hope you get there before it really starts coming down."

Jack said, "You know, Doc, I'd of gone one way or another."

The doctor frowned and shook his head. "Yeah, I know. And if it was me, I'd have done the same thing. Find Dalton before it's too late."

CHAPTER 16

The sled trail up the Chena Valley was well-groomed by travelers to-and-from the hot springs, and miners working Van Curlers Bar at the headwaters of the Chena River.

Jack rested comfortably in the basket, wrapped in a woolen robe. The dogs settled into a ground-eating pace with Corrine driving. There was nothing much to do except ride the runners, and pedal every so often, with long, graceful swings of the leg to help the team on an uphill pull.

Other travelers on the trail this time of night were scarce. The only sounds were the soft padding of the dogs' feet and the light hiss of the runners on the trail. It was amidst this darkened world, this silence and solitude, that Corrine found herself reflecting over the past few days.

Perhaps she had been a little selfish in thinking she could get Dalton's help getting away from her father and the abuse. Jack had been right. Dalton did have a lot on his plate, as Jack had put it.

I shouldn't have expected him to help me. He doesn't even know me. Why should he trust me? In me, I guess he sees my father and The Syndicate. If I were him, I wouldn't trust anyone associated with them, either.

But those eyes! When our eyes met, I thought I was going to melt right then and there. I know he's attracted to me. I felt it. It was as if, for a moment, there was nobody else in the whole room but him and me. I believe he felt the same way.

But oh, I was stupid. I shouldn't have gone to him at the dog barn like I did. I made a fool of myself. Jack tried to warn me, but I wouldn't listen. Dalton had asked me, 'Why don't you just leave?' Well, I guess I just did.

The real reason I didn't leave before was because I was scared, I guess. Scared of what Father might do if he caught me. Well, right now, I don't care. Because Dalton asked Jack to bring me with him when he left the hospital. And now, that's the only thing in the world I care about. Getting to him. Praying to God he's okay. We need to get to Ollie's place.

About twenty-nine mile, on the Chena Valley winter trail they stopped in at the Colorado Roadhouse on Colorado Creek. Jack entered to ask directions to Ollie's trapline trail, while

Corrine took care of the dogs. A few minutes later, Jack returned.

"Well?" Corrine asked.

Jack frowned. "At first, he wasn't none too friendly. Said he didn't like giving out information on folks. I can respect that. Told him that Ollie and I was friends and I had some news for him about Dalton Laird. His eyes sorta lit up and he sez, 'Why didn't you say so.' I sez, 'That's what I'm doin'. He sez he don't know Dalton personally, but he knows *of* him, heard good things about him. He asked me if it was true what he heard about what happened in the Amanita. I sez 'yes, it's true.' He sez, seein' as how he kicked Ward's butt, he'll help us out."

Jack stood there smiling at Corrine for a moment.

"So?" Corrine sounded impatient.

"Oh. Well, he sez there's a sled trail across the winter trail that heads down Colorado Creek to the Chena. We gotta cross the river, then head south along the South Fork. Sez we can't miss it."

* * *

After some searching, they found Ollie's trail. A good foot of fresh powder snow covered the trail. Two old blazes, well-sealed with resin and slashed on the side of a spruce tree marked the beginning of the trail.

It reminded Corrine of her childhood and the games she'd played with the other village children. Games and rhymes not meant merely to entertain, but taught them lessons about surviving in the wilderness.

One such rhyme her grandfather had taught her instilled the old saying, "A blaze, away from camp. Two blazes, towards camp." The two blazes indicated the trail toward Ollie's cabin.

About eight-and-a-half miles later on the South Fork of the Chena, a small cabin at the mouth of Martin Creek loomed out of the darkness. It materialized as a dark blob against the darker vertical lines of spruces, and the dark bluish grays of snowy shadows.

No smoke rose from the chimney and no dogs were in the yard. A brief examination revealed it to be a small line cabin, only used as an overnight shelter.

"His place must be further up river," Jack looked back at Corrine. "You need some rest?"

"No! I don't need any rest. We need to get to Ollie's place as soon as possible and find Dalton."

Jack frowned.

"I know. But the dogs need a good rest. They ain't used to working this hard. There's a good foot-and-a-half of fresh snow they're trying to pull through."

"Jack, we're pushing on. If one or two dogs drop in the trail, then we'll stop. I'll continue on by snowshoe, if need be."

Jack was silent for a bit, then said, "Tell ya what, young'un. You ride the basket and I'll drive. You're lighter than I am and I'll run as much as possible behind the sled."

"But what about your leg and your cracked rib? Remember what the doc said?"

Jack waved her off. "It'll do 'em good. Besides, I need the exercise."

Corrine knew better. *It would be easier on the dogs*, she thought. "Alright. We'll try it your way for a while."

With Jack holding onto the handle bar and jogging behind the sled, they pushed on. It was not long before Corrine became aware of Jack's haggard breathing.

Looking back over her shoulder, she asked, "Jack, you okay?"

"I'll be...alright. I'll rest on the...runners...for a while." He hopped aboard.

"Try peddling. It won't wear you out so fast."

"Young'un," Jack raised his voice, "I've been driving dogs... longer that you are old.... I think I know...what to do."

Corrine turned back around and pulled the fur ruff tighter around her face.

"*Sacre*," she mumbled into the fur. "Just trying to help."

At the mouth of Beaver Creek, Jack stood on the brake and hollered, "WHOA."

The dogs stopped and slumped down in the snow. Between snatching mouthfuls of snow, the dogs panted puffs of steam. Their tongues hung out and flopped over to the side of their frost-covered muzzles as they expelled excess body heat a sure sign to Jack they were worn out.

Jack tied the sled with a snub line to a nearby stunted, black spruce next to the trail. He leaned on the handle bar with both arms and placed his head on his arms, resting. Corrine could tell he was hurting, but she knew he wouldn't admit it. She remained silent.

After a few moments of rest, Jack raised his head and looked at Corrine. "Sorry I snapped at you back there. I apologize."

"I understand," she said. "I guess we're both a little stressed. You want to get there as bad as I do. What do you think we ought to do now?"

"Well, I been cogitatin' on it some. If that feller at Colorado Creek Roadhouse was right, I figure we got no more than five miles to go. I'll strap on the snowshoes and break trail. You give me a thirty-minute head start, then slowly bring the dogs up. They should be pretty rested by then. They rest faster than we do."

Corrine sat in the sled basket, wrapped in the woolen robe. She leaned back against the handle bar and watched as Yukon Jack disappeared into the gloom of night and falling snow.

She knew he must be in a lot of pain. And she marveled at the thought, once again, how he reminded her so much of her grandfather; kindly, strong, showing no weakness and full of knowledge. She yawned then, closed her eyes, and thought about those days that seemed so long ago.

* * *

Corrine awoke with a start. Looking around, she noticed the dogs were tugging on the lead rope and whining. She briefly wondered how long she had been asleep as she threw the snow-covered blanket off herself and climbed out of the sled.

Hope it hasn't been too long.

She decided however long it had been, it was long enough. The dogs were obviously rested. It was time to get moving.

Corrine stood on the break board and untied the snub line from the black spruce. Given the command of "Hike," the dogs dug in and headed up the trail. Corrine rode the break to slow them down. Given the command of "Slow...Slow," the dogs soon settled into a steady trot.

Perhaps she had slept longer than she'd thought. On the other hand, maybe Jack walked faster than she thought he could. Either way, it took a while to catch up to him.

As she approached, she saw him standing off the trail with his hand in the air, indicating her to stop.

"You smell smoke?" he asked.

Corrine sniffed the air. "No. You?"

"I think so. It's hard to tell with this heavy snow coming down. We can't be too far away though. Wait here, I'll go on ahead like before."

Before she could answer, he disappeared into the night.

CHAPTER 17

Her dogs heard it before she did. They became restless, alternating between whining and staring off into the night. Corrine pulled back the fur ruff and listened.

Off in the distance, she heard the barking of sled dogs and knew that Jack must have found Ollie's place. Corrine pulled the snow hook, threw it in the sled, and yelled, "Hike!"

Pulling into the clearing surrounding the cabin, she saw a man whom she assumed to be Ollie standing in the doorway in his red Union Suit, holding a shotgun.

A fog of warm air from the inside of the cabin spilled out of the open doorway and fell upwards into the cold night air.

"What you fellers want dis time o' night?" she heard him demand as she tied the sled to a convenient tree.

"I'm Jack. Better known as Yukon Jack. You visited me in the hospital a few days ago."

Turning around to face the two men, she saw Ollie peer at Jack a few moments then said, "Yeah, so I did." Then, with a wave of his shotgun toward her, he said, "Who dis utter feller?"

With a chuckle, Jack said, "This feller, is Corrine Batiste. Jon Batiste's daughter."

"Jon Batiste's daughter? Yumpin' yimminy, what she doin' out dere? Batiste himself better not be out dere, I'll blast him to kingdom come, I will."

Corrine stepped up to Jack, pulled back the hood of her parka, and said, "Mr. Olson. If you please, I'd like to talk to you and ask your help. It's about Dalton."

A look of concern crossed Ollie's face. "What's wrong wit Dalton?"

"I have reason to believe he may be hurt and needs our help."

"Reason to... how do you know Da..." Ollie stumbled over his words, as he looked first at Jack, then at Corrine then back at Jack.

A voice from inside the cabin said, "Husband! Close door! It getting cold in here."

"Oh. Yes, dear!" Ollie said, over his shoulder. Then to Jack and Corrine, he said, "Yust a moment. I go put some clothes on and help you bed down and feed your dogs."

With the team taken care of, Ollie invited Jack and Corrine to sit at the table and finish what was left of the night's stew and sour-dough biscuits.

Between mouthfuls of food, Jack and Cor-rine both explained what they knew. Ollie sucked on his pipe and contemplated the situation. Ollie's woman sat silently on the bunk bed, repairing a hole in one of Ollie's shirts.

"Well, he has a cabin furder up da Salcha, but I figure he's headed for da Gold Creek cabin. It's a little more secluded, from what Dalton has told me. Batiste may have a hard-er time finding it," Ollie said, after hearing their story.

"Yeah, that's the cabin he told me to get to. Said that's where he'd be. So, you think we can get there before they do?" Jack asked.

Ollie took a couple of puffs from his pipe.

"Don't know. It's at least a t'irty-mile run for us from here. On da udder hand, you're about twenty miles' closer den dey are, by coming up da Chena. We'll be breakin' new trail on da upper end 'til we get on top. It should be a little easier traveling on da wind-swept ridges."

"In that case," Jack said, "I think we should get a little sleep. It'll be sunup in a few hours." He turned to Corrine. "Your dogs aren't used to this much work and I don't want 'em to stove up on us. They could use the rest."

Jack was right, of course. They'd been worked hard after doing nothing all summer.

"Alright," she said reluctantly. "I just wish we were there now. For some reason, I can't see his face when I think about him, and I feel a chill. I know he's still alive, but slipping."

Ollie's Minto Athabaskan woman suddenly looked up at Corrine.

"You have the gift of seeing. Trust it," she said. She held Corrine's gaze with her piercing dark eyes for a couple of seconds and then turned back to her mending, as if to say no more discussion was needed.

Corrine was speechless. It was said her grandmother had had the gift—occasional flashes of insight or feelings most people did not possess. Was it possible Corrine had inherited that ability? It had never crossed her mind before.

As most one-room cabins do, Ollie had a bunk bed in his. Corrine was offered the upper bunk because it was only proper and polite to do so. Since heat rises, the upper bunk would stay warm longer.

Ollie had his woman to keep him warm. They took the lower.

Yukon Jack got the floor by the stove. He took it upon himself to stoke the fire throughout the rest of the night.

Corrine's mind would not slow down. She couldn't help but feel sorry for Jack. He had been through so much the past couple of weeks, and now he had to sleep on the floor. She knew he would be warm under the snow-shoe hare blankets Ollie's wife had made.

Corrine had been concerned about how Jack would make the trip, but she need not have worried, she decided. He told her breaking trail had been good for him. He said he felt the stiffness leave his leg and side. Although he could see out of his left eye, it was still swollen and watered continuously. He turned his head to the left a little so he could see straight ahead. Breaking trail couldn't help that any, only time.

Then, inevitably, her thoughts turned to Dalton.

She hoped he'd made it to his Gold Creek cabin and rested peacefully as the blanket of heavy snow settled over the Northland. If he'd not made it yet, he could be dead or dying out there, somewhere, all alone.

No. He was not dead.

If she truly had the gift, she felt he was alive. He was alive and waiting for her to come to him.

Yes, that was it.

He's waiting for me, waiting...

...and then she was asleep.

* * *

"What time is it?" Corrine asked Jack as they were loading the sleds.

Jack pulled his timepiece from his pocket and looked at it for a bit. "Six twenty-five."

Corrine brushed a wisp of hair from her face with a beaver-fur mittened hand and looked up to the sky.

About another hour and a half to sunrise.

She was anxious to hit the trail.

It had snowed another six inches since they bedded down last night, which made a good three feet total. Corrine was concerned about her sled runners slicing all the way to the bottom and getting bogged down. She said as much to Ollie.

"Yaw, it vood. But da lower trails vere broken a few days ago. Dey got a good bottom to 'em. I got a toboggan sled. Jack and my voman will take da lead and break trail on snowshoe. Then, I vill follow. Dat should pack it down pretty good for you."

Before they were finished packing the sleds, Ollie's woman strapped on a pair of snowshoes, kissed her man good-bye, and disappeared into the swirling snow.

Yukon Jack strapped on his snowshoes. "See you two a little later. When I catch up to your woman, I'll break trail for a spell."

Ollie laughed. "Even vithout your bum leg, you'll never catch up to dat squaw 'less she vants you to. The only t'ing you'll see of dat voman is where she *has* been. She probably half way dere by now."

Jack grinned. "Maybe." Then he, too, turned and disappeared into the swirling snow, following her tracks.

A half hour later, Ollie and Corrine had the loads tied down and the dogs snapped into their tug lines.

Corrine was not sure but it seemed to her that the snow was letting up a little. It was light enough to see the trail, and Ollie took the lead with his toboggan sled. Corrine gave him a few minutes' head start, then pulled the snow hook and gave the command to her dogs. "Hike!"

Although this was no Sunday run with her dogs, Corrine loved the freedom she felt riding the runners of the sled. She reminded herself this was serious business, with Dalton's life at stake.

Earlier, they all had discussed the route and decided to follow Ollie's trapline trail up the South Fork of the Chena to the headwaters. The reasoning was that, since Ollie's trapline was already cleared of brush, all they'd have to do was break trail through the powder snow. It was a relatively short climb from the head-waters to the ridge line that separated the

Chena drainage from the Salcha. It should be easier traveling on the wind-swept ridge line where the snow wouldn't be as deep.

The sun rose behind the lead-gray, overcast clouds that gave birth to little dots of snow which grew larger as they floated gently to earth. They covered the stunted black spruce that grows in the muskeg and permafrost floor of the valley, turning them into upside-down cones of snow. A faint, thin, blue-grey line carved by the snowshoes of Ollie's woman and Jack, bisected the endless white and disappeared into the white horizon in the distance.

Ollie and Corrine followed that faint line and, about an hour later, caught up with Jack. He rode in Ollie's sled until they caught up with Ollie's woman. There, they traded dog teams for snowshoes and Ollie led off with Corrine following. Jack and Ollie's woman rested the dogs and themselves for about an hour. Then they, too, headed up the valley.

They leap-frogged up the valley like this throughout the morning into early afternoon. Corrine noticed Jack was getting worn out from breaking trail. He was a tough old coot, and she knew it irritated him to no end when he finally gave in to her insistence that he drive the sled from then on. She also knew many men half his age would've given up long ago.

The South Fork was only a trickle under the snow as their climb to the ridge line got steeper. The snow had stopped falling earlier, and a breeze kicked up and drove the dull gray clouds away to reveal the intense blue sky above.

Along the ridge line, the wind blew the snow off in swirls that settled along the slopes.

The dazzling bright sun-reflecting snow was hard on the eyes. Snow blindness could soon be a distinct possibility. And, it got colder. A good twenty degrees colder. Without the insulating effect of the cloud cover, the heavy arctic cold settled on the mountains and slid down into the valleys.

When at last they broke out on the ridge top, they were able to make good time. Ollie pointed out "The Butte" to Corrine and Jack about seven miles due east of their present position.

"We have to make it to de back side of dat butte."

From there, Ollie wasn't sure where Dalton's cabin lay. He'd never been in this part of the country before. Always keeping a ridge line or some other natural boundary between himself and other trappers, he'd never ventured too far out of his own territory.

He knew Dalton's cabin was at the mouth of Gold Creek, further east from The Butte. About eight or nine miles, from his reckoning.

Making it to The Butte, they saw a valley to their left, or the north side of the ridge they were on. It extended to the east and then swung south. Surmising this was upper Gold Creek, they stayed on the ridge line and followed it east as far as they could go. Soon, they found themselves looking down into the south facing Gold Creek Valley.

Ollie took out his binoculars and studied the valley below.

Something coal black against the dazzling white background and surrounded by spruce trees caught his eye. Looking closer, he realized a wolf sat in the snow, watching them.

"Yumpin' yimminy..."

"What is it, Ollie?" Corrine asked.

"A black wolf. I t'ink it da one Dalton talk about all da time dat live up here. Da one he bred to his dogs."

"Let me look," Corrine took the glasses from Ollie.

She took a minute to focus the glasses. When the image became sharp, it seemed to her the wolf's eyes were looking into hers through the other end.

"Grandfather..." she said softly.

"Vaut?" Ollie asked.

"Oh, nothing. It's just, that was my grandfather's name. Black Wolf."

"Oh. Okay. Give me dem glasses back," Ollie reached for them.

Looking again into the valley, Ollie made out a ribbon of cleared brush along the creek bottom. He figured it must be a trail of some sort. If it was, it could very well be one of Dalton's trapline trails.

Reaching the creek bottom, they donned snowshoes to break trail through the deeper snow. Crossing the frozen creek, they found where the wolf had been sitting. Not fifteen feet away was a blaze on a spruce tree, indicating the trail.

Corrine's anticipation had been building all day. She was impatient to get to the cabin and Dalton. She clung to the hope he was there and alive.

Yet, veiled by the shadows of her mind was a sense of darkness, and dirt, and pain. What it was, or what it meant, she knew not.

They mushed the last mile down the valley and soon glimpsed a small cabin just ahead, on a bench above the creek. Corrine's heart raced from a mixture of joy and fear. Joy, for soon she would be with Dalton, yet fear for his well-being.

She sensed something was wrong. *Smoke! That's it!* No smoke rose from the chimney. No dogs barked their greeting. Fear pushed joy away and gripped her heart as they pulled up in front of the cabin. The snow was undisturbed.

Corrine ran to the door, pulled the latch-string, and pushed the door in.

"DALTON?" she called.

No answer.

She looked around inside then came back out and gazed into the eyes of Yukon Jack with her own tear-filled, dark brown eyes.

Dalton was not there.

CHAPTER 18

Dalton slowly regained consciousness and realized something heavy was lying on his legs. He couldn't see what it was. He tried moving his legs. The heavy thing wouldn't budge. He tried to reach down and push it off, whatever it was, because it didn't belong there. A searing, burning pain under his left arm caused him to groan. The heavy thing on his legs moved and a cold, wet tongue licked his face.

"Bandit! Is that you girl?"

Bandit whined and licked his face again.

Wait a minute. It's dark. What time is it?

Then, he realized the other dogs were bedded down all around him. One at his head. Others in front of him and others behind him.

A seven-dog night, he mused.

Then, he shivered.

Man, it's cold in here. And this mattress is as hard as a rock. Guess I'll throw some wood on the fire.

He tried to rise up but the searing pain hit him again.

"What the...?"

Reaching over to his left side, he found the source of the pain, sore and sticky wet. Pulling his hand back, he smelled it.

Blood! It smells like...blood!

But, where did the blood come from and why was there so much of it? Briefly, he thought one of the dogs was hurt.

No. I'm the one who's in pain, so I'm the one who's hurt. But how? How did I...

He was groggy, so completely and utterly tired, and cold. If only he could remember.

Dalton grit his teeth and struggled to sit up. As he pulled himself into a seated position, he bumped his head on something. Reaching overhead into the dark, he felt moist earth and rock. Some of it fell into his hair.

"A cave? How did I get in a..."

Dalton gingerly lay back down. Shivering uncontrollably, he tried to remember.

Why am I in here?

Then, the memories bubbled up from his subconscious.

Because it was snowing and I didn't feel well.

No. That wasn't it, exactly. It was snowing all right, but something else was wrong.

I didn't feel well. Why? Because... realization sat in. *...because I've been shot!*

The memory of Hank's face as he sank to his knees in the snow with Dalton's bullet deep in his chest, flashed through Dalton's mind.

Then, he remembered bullets whining through the willows and spraying bits of bark in his face as they smacked the limbs.

He remembered praying to the good Lord that he would make it to the sled. He remembered being concerned about his wound. More than likely, the bullet had missed vital organs, but he couldn't be sure. He hadn't had the time to check it out.

He remembered letting the dogs run where they would because by then, he was so weak he could barely hold onto the sled. He knew Bandit would take them back to the upper cabin.

Twice, he remembered, he'd fallen off the runners of the sled. And twice, Bandit swung the team around to come back to her master. After the second time, Dalton remembered climbing into the basket.

He remembered seeing dead caribou. The skins were taken from them. The red meat and blood scattered across the pure white snow, uncovered by the earlier winds that night. More poisoned bait, with carcasses of wolves and ravens and foxes lying among them.

The next memory to return was that the team had stopped. It was still snowing. The sled had skidded downhill off the trial, sideways, and hung up on a tree. The tree demolished the front curl of the toboggan, rendering it useless.

Dalton remembered a cave, sort of. More like an old bear den about a quarter mile on up the trail. If only he could make it there, he remembered thinking, he could wait out the storm. He hoped the cave wasn't already occupied.

It had taken them about a half hour but he and the dogs finally made it to the den. Dalton had looked for frost buildup around the opening and found none. That was a relief, but just to make sure, he sent Klutina, one of his bigger wheel dogs, in. Soon, she returned and looked at Dalton as if to say, "Well, ya coming in or not?"

Now, lying there, shivering in the dark, Dalton yawned. Trying to recall all that had happened only seemed to make him tired.

He was thankful for what little warmth the dogs gave him and this place to get in out of the weather.

His shivering subsided. He knew what that meant.

I might die here. Nobody knows where I am. I need to get to the cabin. I need to dress this wound. I need...sleep. Just a little sleep.

Bandit whined and nudged Dalton with her muzzle.

Dalton drowsily pushed her away and mumbled, "No...just a little more sleep...then we'll go... Just a little..."

He didn't see her turn and push her way through the snow to the surface.

CHAPTER 19

Somewhere in the misty shadows of his mind, Dalton heard Yukon Jack laughing and talking.

"I wouldn't have done it. No-sir-ee."

I must be losing it, Dalton thought.

Then, another voice faded into his brain, "Dere's yust some t'ings a man can't do."

No... no, that's not Jack. That's Ollie. And why do I faintly smell...what is that? Smoke-tanned buckskin? And something else... something faintly familiar. A woman. That's it. This is crazy. Your brain's playing tricks on you. Just ignore it.

The smell of food cooking overtook the other aromas and pushed the sound of voices from his head. It reminded him of his youth and his mother in the kitchen.

Is this what it's really like to die? he wondered. *Reliving old memories?*

He realized he was no longer cold. In fact, he was downright warm. Something tickled his face. He reached up to brush it away.

Sure glad I have these dogs to keep me warm, he thought.

"Looks like he's starting to come around."

His eyes snapped open.

That sounded like...Corrine!

He realized it wasn't dark anymore. He blinked a few times, trying to adjust to the light.

"Good morning," a female voice said from behind him.

Spinning his head around so fast it gave him a headache, Dalton came face to face with Corrine, snuggled up close.

"What the..." Dalton tried to sit up. The pain from the bullet wound and the pounding in his head hurt so much, he had to lie back down.

Corrine put a hand on his shoulder. "It's okay. For a while there, I thought... we thought we might lose you."

For a moment, Dalton couldn't comprehend what was happening.

Slowly looking around, he realized they were on the top bunk in his cabin. Jack and Ollie, sitting at his table sipping coffee, grinned at him. Ollie's woman was fixing breakfast. She was even looking at him sideways and grinning.

"Hey there, um...big guy. Finally decided to wake up did ya?" Yukon Jack asked with a smile.

Ollie snickered and looked away, while Ollie's woman grinned even more.

"How the heck did you guys...?" His sentence trailed off as he looked back into Corrine's eyes.

She smiled and then bit her upper lip.

Dalton looked back at Jack. Jack and Ollie looked at each other and snickered.

Dalton realized he didn't have any clothes on, and slowly raised the blanket. He looked down at himself.

"I'm nekked under here," Dalton said with a disbelieving voice.

"Nekked as a jaybird," Jack said.

Dalton realized Corrine was under the blanket with him.

Anger and distrust boiled up from deep down inside Dalton. Feelings about women he had tried to keep under control for years. The only thing he could think of was, *This is a setup.*

"WHAT ARE YOU TRYING TO DO TO ME?" he demanded, as he looked from person to person.

Ollie took a puff from his pipe and looked at the door. Jack took another sip of coffee while looking at the ridgepole. Ollie's woman continued to cook breakfast.

Dalton turned his gaze to Corrine with a question he didn't want to ask.

"Don't worry," she said. "I've got my long johns on and nothing happened. Now listen to me, Dalton Laird," she said, like a disapproving mother to an errant child, "We're only trying to save your life."

Dalton looked back at Jack and made eye contact.

Jack finished taking a sip of coffee, then sat the cup on the table.

"You were pretty far gone, partner. We thought you were going to die from exposure. If it hadn't been for Corrine, you probably would've. They ain't no way me or Ollie was going to climb under that blanket with your sorry butt. And Ollie wouldn't have let his woman do it neither. So, you better be glad she's in there keeping you warm."

Well, that makes sense, Dalton told himself. After all, he'd used rocks from the campfire to keep Jack warm a couple of weeks ago. The only rocks around here were in the creek bottom covered with ice and snow.

"Alright," Dalton said, in a more civil tone. "But how did you find me?"

173

"It was that lead dog of yours, Bandit," Jack said. "After we got to the cabin last night and found that you weren't here, we were trying to decide what to do.

"Next thing I know, Bandit is sitting under a tree over yonder. I called to her. I guess she recognized my voice because she came right up to me. Anyway, we followed her tracks and she led us back to you."

"Where is she now?"

"She's layin' down there under the bunk," Jack said, with a toss of his head.

Dalton leaned over, looked down toward the bottom bunk, and saw Bandit's head resting comfortably on her paws.

"Good girl," Dalton said. "The only female I could ever trust." Then, looking back at Jack and Ollie, he asked, "How're the rest of the dogs?"

"Oh, dey yust fine," Ollie said. "Fed and bedded down. The t'ree of you yust lay dere and heal up, big guy."

"The three of us?" Dalton looked over at Jack.

"Yeah, you, Corrine... and whatever you call that thing you got with ya."

Ollie snorted smoke out his nose and choked, then coughed while Ollie's woman snickered and looked sideways at Dalton, then quickly back to what she was doing.

Dalton glanced at Corrine and she was, again, biting her upper lip, evidently trying to suppress a smile.

It slowly dawned on Dalton what they were having so much fun at his expense about.

He felt his face go flush, then he stammered, "Did... did you *all* see...? Oh man!"

"Couldn't help it, partner. He had to get those wet clothes off you, patch up that bullet hole and get you under those blankets," Jack said.

At first, Dalton felt anger well up inside him. His first impulse was to climb out of bed, hitch up the dogs, and leave.

On second thought, he'd had enough of the cold for a while. Besides, he *had* asked Jack to bring Corrine with him, and her nearness was rather nice.

He decided it wasn't a bad thing after all.

CHAPTER 20

While they mushed from Fairbanks to Dalton's main cabin on No Grub Creek, Batiste mulled the whole situation over.

No one had caused him so much grief as Dalton had. He'd heard talk around town before of this Dalton Laird, and so knew *of* him. But when Dalton entered the Amanita that day, Batiste knew he was someone different.

Batiste thought his daughter had probably thought so, too. It hadn't escaped his attention that day in the Amanita—her interest in him nor Dalton's interest in her, though brief as it was.

No, Dalton was not one to be trifled with. Dalton pushed back, and Batiste was not used to that. It was impressive the way Dalton had handled Ward and pinned his ear to the table with his own knife. Now, as his own men were setting up their tents in the clearing just outside the main cabin, Batiste wished they were half the man Dalton was.

Yes, Dalton had taken a bullet. When he kicked back the two feet of newly fallen snow and uncovered crimson stains at the edge of the clearing, Batiste saw for himself where Dalton had fallen.

Nevertheless, was Dalton dead, like Frank and some of the other men thought? Batiste did not believe it. Dalton was too good an outdoorsman. He knew how to take care of himself. Batiste had a gut feeling Dalton had holed up out there, somewhere, like a wounded grizzly, waiting for the right moment.

Batiste had successfully pushed Dalton out of the lower Salcha Valley, and he was confident he could hold that ground. But he wanted more. He wanted the upper Salcha as well. More ground, more furs. Batiste knew if Dalton wasn't eliminated, he would cause problems.

Dalton's words came back to haunt him, 'I'll fight ya for it.'

Batiste decided the best thing to do was to track Dalton down and eliminate the threat. The vast interior of Alaska could swallow a man and not a trace would be found. Who's to say that couldn't happen to Dalton? There had to be line cabins further up the river, and more than likely Dalton had holed up in one of them.

Batiste opened the door of the cabin. "WARD!"

"YEAH, BOSS?" Ward hollered back from somewhere across the clearing.

"Get in here."

"What's up, Boss?" Frank Ward entered the cabin.

"Close the door and have a seat."

Ward closed the door, then crossed the room and sat at the table.

Batiste paced the floor a couple of times, then, turning to Ward, said, "It's because of the incompetence of you and your men, I find that I have to take matters under control, no?"

"What?"

"Just shut up and listen. I want you to leave two men here to guard this place and skin those furs we got between here and the lower cabin off the bait piles. The rest of the men need to pack up and hook up the dogs. The sun'll be up soon and I want to be on the trail when it rises."

"But, Boss..."

"What?" Batiste asked impatiently, pulling a cigar out of his shirt pocket.

"They've spent all night driving the dogs hard to get here. The dogs are tired and so are the men. They just finished setting up their tents and haven't even had time to eat."

Sacre...That's always been your problem Ward, Batiste thought, as he bit off the end of the cigar and spit it onto the floor.

"Ward. You're soft, no?" Batiste punched a hole in the air with the cigar at Ward. "Always wanting people to like you. Well, I couldn't care less about those dogs right now, or the men for that matter. Dalton is my concern. He's going to fight me until one of us is dead and I aim to make sure it's him.

"Now, we're going to find his trail and track him down. He's got to be holed up in a cabin somewhere. It can't be that hard. Now get a move on."

Batiste watched Ward's face go flush and his eyes narrow. Standing up from the chair, Ward walked to the door and went out.

Batiste started to put the cigar in his mouth but realized his jaws were hurting. He had a habit of clinching his teeth together when he was upset. Placing the cigar back in his shirt pocket, he made a mental decision to relax his jaw muscles. He worked them back and forth a couple of times.

Batiste waited a few minutes for the word to circulate among the men, then he pulled on his wolf-skin parka and the damp mittens that had been hanging above the stove to dry.

He said to no one, "Well, time to face the music."

As he stepped out onto the porch, a low murmur and grumbling came from the men.

It stopped as soon as they noticed him standing there. An uneasy truce filled the air. This brought a smile to Batiste's face.

"*Oui*, grumble men. It's because of Dalton Laird we do this thing, no? The sooner we take care of him, the sooner we can rest easy. And the more money we make." He hoped to turn their anger towards Dalton.

Grudgingly, it seemed, the men turned to their tasks.

Instead of the usually excited barking and jumping up and down at the end of their chains when the men began packing the sleds, the dogs remained silent. Some wagged their tails and looked on, perhaps hoping for a handout or a friendly pat on the head. The rest stayed curled up, their noses covered by their tails in an attempt to keep warm. Most offered no resistance as they were dragged unceremoniously into place and harnessed into the tug lines.

At eight o'clock, just as the sun peeked over the southeastern horizon, they pulled their snow hooks and headed up the river. About five miles later, they passed the moose quarter that Ward, Hank, and the Swede had poisoned, and that Dalton had found.

Batiste was pleased to see what looked like several foxes, a wolverine, and three or four dead wolves.

He hollered back over his shoulder, "Someone gather up those furs. We'll skin them out later."

He watched as one of the sleds pulled to the side.

He also noticed one of the drivers shake his head and look away from the scene of death as he drove by, but dismissed it from his mind. He had other things to think about, and he wondered if there were some mink and ermine mixed in there as well. He hoped so, for they would fetch a handsome price back East.

Another torturous ten miles passed under their runners. The trail had no bottom to it and all the men, except Jon Batiste, took turns breaking trail on snowshoes.

At the mouth of Upper Boulder Creek, they came to a cabin. It was obvious no one had been there in quite some time.

Ward wadded through the snow to Batiste's sled.

"Boss, there ain't nobody here. No sign anywhere. I think he's laying out there, dead somewhere."

Batiste smiled and looked around.

"No Ward. He ain't dead. He's out there somewhere, very much alive, just biding his time. He had to have left the Salcha somewhere," he said thoughtfully. Batiste couldn't help but admire the man for hiding his trail so well. Of course, all the new snow had helped.

The only thing Batiste could think to do was to backtrack and keep a closer eye on anything unusual that might indicate where Dalton had left the main trail. It was two thirty in the afternoon. By his calculation, that would give them about two-and-a-half hours before sunset. That was a concern, but the trail was broke and well-packed, so the return trip would be faster.

"Ward, turn the teams around. We're heading back. Tell 'em to keep a sharp eye out for anything unusual. Anything that may indicate where Dalton left the trail."

It took some fancy talking on Ward's and Batiste's parts to get the men to backtrack. Most of them wanted to stay where they were to rest the dogs and hunt fur. Eventually, Batiste won out. Tempers flared. The men cursed and argued. The dogs howled in pain as whips licked out, trying to untangle the teams as they were turned around.

At the mouth of the North Fork, they had their first real trouble with the dogs. One of the teams up ahead lay down in the middle of the trail and wouldn't budge.

"What's the trouble up there?" Batiste

hollered. He pulled his team to a stop with the others.

Somebody answered back, "One of the teams quit on us. We can't get 'em to move."

"*Sacre...*" Batiste uttered under his breath. He stomped the snow hook into the trail.

Taking the dog whip he always carried on his sled, he waded through the snow up to the offending team and beat the dogs. Through his fury and rage, and through the whining and whimpering of the beaten dogs, one icy cold voice made its way to Batiste's brain and stopped him in mid-swing.

"Stop, I say, or by gum I'll run ya through."

Batiste turned, still holding the whip in the air. He saw Gee pole Larson crouched with his feet shoulder-width apart and holding a Bowie knife low, cutting edge up.

Their eyes locked.

"You lay the whip to my dogs again and I'll lay ya open, that's a fact. Nobody beats my dogs."

Batiste thought about the whip in his hand, already raised and ready for action. Batiste could see Gee pole meant every word, and Batiste had no doubt Gee pole knew how to use that knife.

Lowering his arm, Batiste looked around at the other teams.

Raising his voice, he said, "Boys! We've got Dalton on the run and we're close, I can feel it! I know you're cold and tired. So am I. But, we have a chance to make millions... millions, I say, in furs. And I swear by my poke, I'll give another thousand to the man who kills Dalton Laird!"

Batiste smiled within himself as he watched the men's approving nods and heard mumbling up and down the line.

"It'll be dark soon. We'll camp here for the night. You men get some rest, you'll need it!"

Batiste headed back to his sled. He caught the icy stare of Gee pole Larson. They held each other's gaze for a moment, and then Batiste felt a chill like melting snow water run down his spine. Gee pole grinned and Batiste noticed he had a couple of teeth missing from gums beginning to turn black from the effects of scurvy.

"I think maybe I get that thousand, one way or the other," Gee pole said.

Gee pole replaced the Bowie in its sheath and turned away. Batiste exhaled a breath of relief and walked back to his sled.

Batiste dug his tin cup out of the sled bag and told Ward to take care of the dogs.

"I'm going down to the river to get a drink of water and think a bit."

At the riverbank, Batiste found an open lead, knelt down, and dipped his cup into the crystal-clear waters of the upper Salcha.

As he sipped the icy cold water, his eyes scanned the opposite shoreline, taking in all that was there while his brain pieced it all together.

All his years of living in the wilderness and all of his life's experiences came together and soon, his brain told him that what he was looking at was not quite right. Jon Batiste smiled as he realized that the low angle of the sun, cast shadows that showed the slightest indentation under the new snow.

Stretching from one bank to the other was the indentation of a track left by a toboggan sled. If the sun had been at a different angle, he would have missed it completely.

Following the track with his eyes to the brush on the opposite bank, he saw a spruce with two scars scabbed over with pitch.

Ward came up behind him. "Boss, you want anything to eat?"

"Later."

"Okay."

"Ward?"

"Yeah, Boss?"

"I found his trail."

CHAPTER 21

Yukon Jack had rummaged through the cabin and cache while Dalton lay passed out under the blankets with Corrine. Jack found an extra set of clothes for Dalton to wear.

After he awoke, Dalton managed to put the clothes on while under the blankets, in spite of the stiffness and pain. He gingerly made his way to the table and sat down with Jack and Ollie. Corrine got dressed while they talked.

"Well, now. Batiste has possession of your cabins and trapline. What do you plan to do about it?" asked Jack.

"I don't know." Dalton accepted a cup of tea from Ollie's woman. "All I ever wanted was to be left alone. Fairbanks has grown so big, I feel jittery when I'm there. And now big mining companies are moving in and pushing the small miner out. There're so many people around anymore it's gettin' to where a man can't spit without hitting someone else. I miss the good old days."

"It's called progress." Corrine walked up to the table.

Ollie stood up. "Here. Take my seat. I go stand by da stove. Dees old bones need da heat."

"Thank you, Ollie." She accepted the chair and sat down.

"Progress? Well, whatever it's called, I don't like it," said Dalton.

Corrine accepted a cup of tea. "Whether we like it or not, things change. Nothing stays the same. Some of it's good, some bad. My people most of all, have had to change a lot these past few years."

Dalton leaned both forearms on the table, cupped his tea in both hands, looked at her, frowned, and then sipped his tea.

She is right, of course, he thought. He'd watched Fairbanks grow in just six or seven years from a wilderness trading post run by E.T. Barnett on the banks of the Chena, to a boom town complete with electricity, telephones, and running hot and cold water. But he didn't have to like it.

Progress, he knew, brought the bad along with it. The followers, the riff-raff, the pimps, and highwaymen - that was a different story. The U.S. Marshal had been transferred to another district, and Fairbanks, lying within District Three that covered most of the northern half of Alaska, waited for his replacement.

They had a Chief Deputy Marshal and a Deputy in Fairbanks, with a couple more Deputies scattered around the outlying gold camps. Way too much work to be concerned about a trapline dispute.

Dalton looked down at his teacup.

"Maybe I'll just let him have this valley. Move on to somewhere else. The Fortymile country maybe or Black Rapids. I always liked that place."

"So, you're just going to up and quit, huh?" Jack asked. "Just like that? Never thought I'd see the like."

Dalton looked up and saw a look of disbelief on Jack's face.

"Well, it ain't worth it. One man's dead. They left you to die out there all alone. And I nearly bought the farm, myself. If they want it that bad, they can have it."

"You sure ain't acting like the man I always heard you were," Jack said half disgustedly. He crossed his arms.

"Yeah? Well. That'll teach ya to believe everything ya hear." Dalton sat upright and stiff, and tried to stare a hole through Jack's eyes.

"Gentleman, please," Corrine interjected. "Must we argue right now?"

Dalton looked at her, then slunk back down in his chair and looked at his teacup again, embarrassed at the realization they were both acting childish.

"Sorry," Dalton said. "I'm just sore, hungry, and tired of it all."

"Yeah, I'm sorry too," Jack said. "All I was trying to say was, somebody needs to stand up to Batiste, and I think you're the man to do it. That's all.

"I am kinda disappointed to hear you talk about quitting, though. Oh, by the way, Deputy Dreibelbis stopped by the hospital a couple of days ago and asked me to give a letter to you. It's in my parka, I'll get it."

Jack got up crossed over to where his parka hung on a nail by the door, and dug through the pockets. Pulling an envelope out of the inside pocket, he returned to the table and sat down.

"Here it is." Jack tossed it on the table in front of Dalton.

Dalton picked it up, looked at it, and asked, "Did he say what it was about?"

"No, he didn't. He just said to give it to you, and that it was important."

Dalton opened the envelope and read the letter. After he was finished, he laid it down on the table.

"Well, that changes everything."

"So...what does it say?" Jack didn't hide his impatience.

Corrine picked up the letter and read it aloud.

"*Know Ye: That reposing special trust and confidence in the patriotism, integrity and ability of Dalton Laird, I, Judge James A. Wickersham, in pursuance of and by virtue of authority vested in me, do appoint him U.S. Deputy Marshal of the Third Judicial District of Alaska, until such time as his service is no longer needed.*"

Ollie slapped his leg and laughed.

"Vell, I'll be a suck-egg mule. Now ya got da law behind ya to do somet'ing about it, by grannies."

Dalton looked at him sideways.

"Maybe. Maybe not."

"What do ya mean?" Jack's face wore a look of concern.

"What I mean is, there's no law that says a man can stake a claim on trapping territory like there is for miners. Trappers simply operate under an unwritten code of ethics that say if someone is already trapping a certain place, you find someplace else to trap. They don't have to. It's just common courtesy."

"You sayin' that if Batiste wants to trap the Salcha Valley, he can?"

"That's what I'm saying."

"Well, if that don't beat all." Jack shook his head.

Dalton watched Jack take another sip of tea then stare at the floor for a moment.

Jack raised his head.

"What about your cabins and all your equipment? Don't that count for something?"

"Under the homestead laws, I guess I could charge him with criminal trespass. But he'd be out of jail in six months."

The cabin fell silent then as everyone became lost in his or her own thinking.

"What about the murder in Minto?" Corrine asked.

"There're no witnesses. It's just hearsay. Rumor," Dalton said.

From the other end of the cabin, a voice said, "I saw it."

Everyone turned and looked at Ollie's woman.

"What did you say?" Dalton asked, not believing his ears.

"I saw it," she repeated.

"You saw it happen? Why didn't you say something?"

"*Gesek* not believe Indian. They don't care Indian got killed."

Dalton hesitated a few moments, remembering some of the things her people had been through.

"Well, that may have been true in the past. But things have changed, and, as Corrine pointed out, some for the good. If you tell me what you saw, I'll arrest his butt and drag it to jail. You've got to promise me though, you'll tell the court everything you tell me. Can you do that?"

Ollie's woman was silent for a moment, then nodded her head. "Yes."

"Good. Now, what happened?"

She furrowed her eyebrows and looked down at the floor as if thinking about what or how to say it.

"One winter ago, I visit my family in Minto. Father is old. Mother sent me out to my brother's trapline with food and to make sure he alright. When I mush up to cabin, I hear *gesek*... um, white man hollering. I get closer and see Batiste with furs and my brother arguing. Then, I hear a gunshot and my brother fall down. Batiste, he leave. I find my brother with a bullet in *bets'eega*'...um, his guts. I try to doctor him, but he die anyway."

Silence again filled the tiny cabin, as each was lost in thought.

Dalton looked at Corrine and saw a tear rolling down her cheek. He felt a stab of pain, strangely, somewhere in his chest.

She's a remarkable woman. So proud and strong and beautiful.

Then, reaching across the table, he brushed her tear away.

She looked at him.

"I...I know my father is a hard man. And I hate the way he treats me and his men. I've often wondered about my mother, and if Father was capable of murder. I never wanted to believe it. I think Grandfather, *Zhoh Zhraii,* knew. I think Grandfather banished Father from Fort Yukon. Either that or Father fled, afraid for his own life, and took me with him. I don't think I'll ever know what happened for sure."

Jack took Corrine's hand.

"We may never know what happened to your ma, young'un, but at least we can try to do something about the murder in Minto."

Corrine gave Jack the briefest of smiles, then, rose and moved to the frost-covered window and looked out into years gone by.

Dalton decided he was tired of ending up with the short end of the stick. Now that he had the law on his side, he was going to do something about it. He could bring some peace back into his life and resolution in the lives of others. And when that was done, he could get on with living the way he wanted, alone and free.

Although the alone part was beginning to eat on him a little. Exactly what he was going to do, he wasn't sure.

He knew that whatever it was, he couldn't do it alone.

He'd need help.

CHAPTER 22

"Jack, I want you to take Ollie and his wife back to town and give a deposition to Dreibelbis. Take Corrine with you. They don't need to be around if Batiste shows up. Tell Dreibelbis what's going on and tell him I'm going to need his help bringing Batiste in. With Batiste out of the picture, the rest of the Syndicate should disband and drift on. I'll heal up here for a day or two 'til you get back."

"Oh, no you don't," Corrine said. "I'm staying right here with you."

Dalton turned to her with a surprised look on his face.

"Don't look at me like that. I've nothing left for me in Fairbanks. Besides, what if you break open a stitch or something? And you're going to need some decent food in you if you're going to heal up properly."

Dalton was speechless. She was right, of course. Obviously, she'd taken his advice and left it all behind. But, dang it all, he certainly didn't mean to put her in harm's way.

Never-the-less, it would be comforting to have her company and cooking...for a while. But just for a while.

"All right," he said reluctantly. "Just don't get any ideas any of this means anything."

"Why, Dalton Laird. Whatever do you mean?"

Dalton sighed. "Nothing."

Looking at Jack, he said, "Can you drive Corrine's dogs to town with your bum leg?"

"Yeah, I think so. I drove 'em part of the way here."

"Good. When can you and Ollie leave?"

Jack looked at Ollie and shrugged his shoulders. "Within an hour?"

"Yeah, I t'ink so," Ollie said.

Dalton nodded his head. "Good. The sooner you leave, the sooner you'll get back."

***

Corrine waved them goodbye from the cabin door, then turned her attention to Dalton. He was lying on the bottom bunk, and it was time to change the dressing on his bullet wound.

As she bathed his wound with warm water, she remembered that day in the dog livery when she had met Dalton, alone. She had gone there, willingly, on her own. Something a lady just doesn't do. However, she was never one for convention and thought white women were too repressed anyway.

Looking back, she didn't really know for sure why she went there.

Perhaps, I thought he would sweep me off my feet, like some gallant knight in far off England.

He'd rejected her and it was painful, but then he'd sent that telegram to Jack asking him to bring her with him.

He is changing his mind. Call it intuition, if you will.

Intuition.

Ollie's woman had told her she had the gift of "seeing." Corrine hadn't really thought about it much. She recalled stories some of the Elders used to tell about her grandmother and how she could see things others could not. Was it just, 'intuition' after all?

"Your mind seems to be a hundred miles away," Dalton said.

With a start, Corrine was thrust into the present. Quickly looking up at Dalton, then back down at her work, she blushed.

"Oh, just wondering." She got up and carried the pan of warm, bloody wash water to the table.

"Wondering what?"

"What brings a man like you to the north?" She sat down in a chair.

"Shouldn't we put another bandage on this?" Dalton asked.

"It needs some air. Dry out a little. So, like I said, what brings you to the north?"

Dalton was silent a bit, and then said, "No signs."

Corrine was confused. "No signs?"

"Yeah, you know? Signs. Like 'no trespassing', or 'private property', or 'keep out', don't do this, or don't do that. This is wide-open God's country. On a clear day, you can see the old White Mountain...the tall one. What do your mother's people call it?"

"My mother's people don't have a word for it. Ollie's woman's people call it *Deenadheet*."

"Yeah, that's it. On a clear day, you can see *Deenadheet* over two hundred miles away. A man can travel any direction from here and see things that probably no other white man has ever seen. That's something. Kind of like the old west used to be.

"Nowadays, you can't hardly go anywhere in the states without permission. I sure hope Alaska don't get like that. It just wouldn't be right, somehow."

Corrine watched him as he spoke. She

loved to listen to him talk, she realized. Moreover, she loved the sparkle in his eyes when he felt passionate about something like Alaska.

Nevertheless, she found it hard to comprehend what it was like in the states, for she had never been there. She didn't understand why he felt this way. She thought there might be more to it.

Corrine gathered up new bandages and walked back to the bunk.

"That may have lured you to Alaska, but what caused you to leave your home to come here?" She laid out the supplies she would need.

Dalton frowned and looked away.

Corrine felt concerned.

"Is that a, how you say... touchy subject?"

Dalton looked back at her and slowly nodded his head. Then, he winched slightly as she dabbed alcohol on the wound.

"Sorry," she said, as she looked up at him.

Dalton looked down at her.

"For what? Askin' me personal questions or burnin' me with the alcohol?"

Corrine looked away, embarrassed. What right did she have pressing into his business, anyhow?

"Both, I guess."

"Well, no harm done. Fact is, it was a woman. A woman I thought I'd spend the rest of my life with."

Corrine watched his jaw muscles tighten and bulge.

"What happened?"

Dalton's eyes drifted from her and focused on nothing as if looking into yesterday. His jaw relaxed.

He looked back at her, and said, "We were married after a whirlwind romance. I was convinced we were meant to be together. Looking back, I guess I should have known something was wrong. I used to catch her lying to me. She'd lie to cover up one lie, then lie to cover up that one.

"She wasn't very loving, criticized everything I did for her. It seemed like nothing was ever good enough. I figured that was just her personality and I had to learn to live with it. I thought deep down she really loved me but didn't really know how to show it.

"Then she began to make little hints in passing about separation and divorce. I dismissed them at first. I didn't believe in divorce. I believed once married always married. Then one day, while I was out of town on business, she borrowed money from the neighbors and just up and left. Went back to her mother.

"I did a lot of crying alone at night and begging her in letters to come back home. She did. But as soon as she got back she told me she didn't love me and had never loved me. I asked her why she married me if she was never in love with me. She said I was a convenient way to get away from her parents and see new country.

"I was devastated the second the words left her mouth. It felt like someone had shot an arrow through my heart. She stayed for a few more years, but she kept talking about divorce and how she was never happy.

"I got her to go with me and talk to the pastor of our church. But she didn't like what he told her and refused to go back.

"Then one day, she up and left again. I asked her if there was any way we could work it out. And she said, 'no.' I was so emotionally drained from trying to hold my marriage together, I didn't put up a fight. I decided I had some pride and I wasn't going to grovel and beg like I did the last time she'd left. I surrendered and gave her the divorce she wanted. Funny thing was, it gave me peace... there was no pain.

"Later, when it came due, I found she had somehow forged my name to a two-thousand-dollar loan at the bank. Then, I found out she had ruined my character in the community and my own family by spreading rumors. She told people that I was treating her badly and that I was running around with other women. I found out she even went so far as to tell our friends and family she was concerned about their children when I was around them.

"Can you believe a person would stoop that low to try to hurt you? Being in law enforcement and a regular churchgoer, you can understand what that did to my credibility. Not only did she ruin my character, but she ruined my job as well. Nobody ever came to me to talk about it—to ask my side of the story. And I'm not one to go around complaining about my lot in life. Anyway, I had to get out of there. Away from the lies, from the memories."

"As a woman, I can tell you women are very vindictive. But I just don't understand a person who would do something like that."

Corrine finished wrapping the wound with a clean bandage.

"I guess I never understood her, either," Dalton said.

Corrine washed her hands in the hot water on the stove.

"So, did you ever think of remarrying?"

Dalton gave a snort of disgust.

"Remarrying? I'd sooner kick a momma grizzly in the butt and run off with her cub. I haven't let myself get that close to a woman since. I could do without that kind of heart-ache, let me tell ya. They're all the same."

That stung a little. Corrine turned and faced him while drying her hands on a towel. "So, you think all women are the same?"

"Well, no, I didn't mean it like that exactly I guess, it's just…"

"Just what?"

"I don't know. I guess I just don't want to take the chance."

Corrine hung up the towel.

"Take the chance of what? Getting hurt again? Dalton, I believe if we find someone who truly loves us for who and what we are, it makes all those hurts we went through to find that person worth it."

Dalton looked at her with a blank look on his face. "Who made you an expert in such matters?"

Corrine sat down at the table. "Well, nobody. It's just that things change and there's nothing you can do about it. You just have to accept it and move on. Quit living in the past."

She watched as a frown crossed his face.

"Living in the past? I ain't living in the past. I'm living right now. I get up when I want. I go where I want. And I make a living on my own terms. I live or die by my own decisions. I'm happier now than I've ever been."

"Are you really?"

"Well...yeah."

Corrine studied him a minute and decided he didn't sound very convincing.

"I think you feel there's something missing, and you can't quite put your finger on it."

Dalton sighed deeply, looked up at the ceiling and back at her.

"Okay, Miss Expert. What would that be?"

Corrine smiled. "The love of a good woman. Something you thought you had once but didn't. You don't know what it's truly like to be loved."

Dalton sat silent for a minute, picking at some fur on the blanket.

"Well, I'll admit that I have a lot of time to think about things out here in the Great Alone, and sometimes I think about how different things could have been. Then, I think I'm just jinxed. I'm destined to be one of those guys who'll never find a good woman and die alone like Moose Johnson did last summer up on the Goodpasture."

Corrine was getting frustrated. Was he ever going to see she was the woman for him?

Standing up, she said, "Dalton Laird, you're not jinxed. You just wouldn't know a good woman if she were standing in front of you!"

"What's that supposed to mean?" he asked, with a tone of astonishment.

Corrine stood there for a minute, hoping he would catch on. He didn't, and it didn't look like he was going to.

"Oh, you make me so frustrated."

"What? Why?"

Corrine pulled her mukluks on and took her parka off the nail. After opening the door, she looked back at Dalton. "Just think about it." She stepped outside and closed the door behind her.

Why do men have to be so thick-headed? I know he wants me. I see it in his eyes. He just won't admit it.

She loaded up her arms with firewood.

CHAPTER 23

That night, the temperature dropped. The intense cold frosted the inside of the windowpane from the breath of the sleeping man and woman with a quarter inch of intricate geometric designs. The log walls of the cabin slowed the advancing cold but they could never stop it. It probed and tested every crack for a chinkless opening and spilled down the cold chimney like a waterfall.

Dalton was the first to waken, and he lay there listening to the deafening silence of an Alaskan winter. Ever so faintly, he could hear Corrine's rhythmic breathing in the bunk above him. He was pleased.

Quietly, so as not to awaken her, Dalton dressed and went outside to relieve himself. As he shut the door behind him, he noticed the thermometer on a nearby tree read twenty-seven below. Then, looking up, he saw the northern lights... and he watched.

Mesmerized, he couldn't help but feel

his life was like those lights, blown about by some cosmic wind, forcing them to sway, ever-changing overhead in shades of blues, greens, and yellows, some tinged with red. And he found himself wondering, like the thousands of times before, where they came from and where they went. Then, like the thousands of times before, he decided he probably would never know, and such things were better left to mystery.

As Dalton gathered an armload of wood, he thought about what Corrine had said.

Why do women have to be so... so bewildering? Another mystery mankind will probably never figure out. And what did she mean, exactly, by I 'wouldn't know a good woman if she were standing in front of me'? I think I'd know a good woman when I saw one. Mr. Munson's wife is a good woman. Ollie's wife is a good woman. Corrine's a good woman and she was standing in front...

At that moment, somewhere in the dark, boreal forest, a Great Horned Owl called out its lonely woes, searching for its mate. Further off in the distance, another owl answered. And, as the lonesome sound pierced his inner being, Dalton suddenly knew Corrine was right. He would never truly be happy without a woman in his life. And, he suddenly knew, he could never live with himself if he let Corrine get away.

Later that morning, Dalton sat in the chair in his long johns, while Corrine knelt beside him and cared for his wound. Things were a little quiet between them, each lost in their own thoughts. She tenderly washed and dressed his wound, then gathered the supplies together and stood up.

"Looks like you're going to live," she said, matter-of-factly.

"Thanks to you, I feel a bunch better."

"I'll wash up and fix breakfast."

They shared breakfast the same way, very little talk. Dalton thought several times about opening up the conversation they'd had the night before but decided the time was not right. When they were through eating, Corrine put more wood on the fire, pulled on her mukluks and parka, and then went outside. Dalton lay down on the lower bunk. No sooner than he began to relax, Corrine burst through the door. He could see by the look on her face that something was wrong.

"Men coming!" she blurted out.

"Where?" Dalton sat up and reached for his pants.

"Down the valley. I was going to feed the dogs when I noticed they were interested in something down there. So, I listened and I heard far off men cursing and yelling. Like white men driving dogs."

Dalton paused, thought a bit, then resumed putting on his pants.

"It's got to be Batiste," he said. "He must've found my trail. I was afraid of that."

Standing up to put his shirt on, he grunted a little as the pain in his side burned like fire.

"Careful Dalton, you're going to start bleeding again. Here, let me help you."

Corrine picked up his shirt and held it open as Dalton put his arms into the sleeves. Then she stepped in front of him to help with the buttons. For a moment, as they stood face to face, their eyes met and Dalton felt all the cares and pain slip away. He wanted so much to pull her close and kiss her passionately. But, he didn't.

Dalton pulled on his snow boots and stepped outside into the cold, still air to listen.

They're breaking trail through three feet of fresh powder snow. They've got about a half hours' worth of work before they make the cabin.

Stepping back inside, he told Corrine, "They're about thirty minutes away, which means we got no more than fifteen to pack and go. You think you can do that while I harness the dogs?"

"We'll never make it," she said, shaking her head.

"They're going to be dog-tired when they reach the cabin, and they're going to want to rest. My team's fresh. Theirs aren't. We can easily outdistance them."

"Dalton, listen to me. You don't know my father. He will push his men to keep going. Besides, you don't have a sled. Yours got busted up when you got away from Ward in the gunfight. Remember?"

Dalton was stunned. Trying to think back on that night, he realized there was a lot missing in his memory. The only thing he could remember was falling into the sled basket when he was too weak to hang on to the handlebar, and waking up in some kind of cave or something, then, after that, waking up in his cabin.

"No... I forgot about the sled."

"We found it beside the trail, not too far from where we found you. We got your rifle, snowshoes and pack from the sled, the tug line and the harnesses and stashed them in the cache."

Dalton thought a bit. "Well, I guess we'll use the snowshoes. There should be an extra pair in the cache. We can use them to get away. I don't know if I'll be able to hold them off long enough till Jack gets back with Dreibelbis."

Corrine took Dalton by the hand, looked him in the face.

"You go. I'll stay here. Father doesn't know I'm here. It will surprise and confuse him. I can try to detain him as long as I can while you make tracks."

She's right, of course, he thought. *She'd never be able to stay ahead of them on snowshoes. Without her, I have a chance. But...*

"I don't want to leave you...behind, that is. I'll stay. We'll face this together."

Corrine smiled. "Alright," she said, and kissed him on the cheek.

"Now, the first thing we need to do is stack firewood around the walls, no telling how long we'll be pinned down in here. We'll need extra food too, just in case. You get the food and whatever you think we might need out of the cache. I'll stack the wood and cut gun ports in the walls."

Dalton donned his parka and mittens and headed out the door. Corrine headed for the cache and Dalton for the woodshed.

Dalton stacked two rows of wood, end to end, along one wall with a space between them, just wide enough for one person to reach the wall. He was just finishing when Corrine entered with an armload of food, blankets, and other things.

"Did ya happen to find any ammo?"

"Yeah, two boxes," she said.

"Good. Hope it will be enough."

211

"Where do you want me to put this stuff?"

"On the top bunk," he said. Then, quickly looking over his work, "We don't have time for more wood. This will have to do. Step outside and fetch me the bow saw hanging by the door. There should be a wood chisel on the bench, also."

Dalton removed his parka and mittens as Corrine retrieved the tools. Taking the blade from the bow saw, he wrapped one end with a piece of leather and bound it on with a strip of cloth for a makeshift handle.

Taking the chisel, he feverishly began notching the top edge of the second log from the floor, between the two stacks of wood. Making a hole all the way through to the outside, he was able to get the saw blade in and cut down to the top of the first log.

Doing the same thing about six inches to the right, he knocked out the piece of log, which made a gun port big enough to cover most of the clearing from the southwest, to the southeast. Doing the same thing on the front wall by the door, he and Corrine could effectively cover all of the clearing from the southeast, his trail coming up from the North Fork to the northwest, and the trail leading to Ollie's place.

Corrine kept watch from the first gun port, and as Dalton finished up the second one, said, "They're here."

Dalton stood up and watched through the window by the door as Batiste gestured for his men to spread out in the tree line along the creek below the bench. Dalton dug in his shirt pocket for his Copenhagen, took a pinch, put it away, then levered a round in his rifle as he contemplatively watched their movements.

Turning back to Corrine, he said, "Turn that table up-side-down and put it on the bottom bunk. Under the table is a trap door to the root cellar. If they start laying down a hail of bullets, you and Bandit get in there quick. The logs will stop most of 'em, but a lucky few will get through the chinking. Hopefully, the firewood will stop those but I ain't countin' on it."

Looking back out the window, Dalton saw Batiste walk up to the door in his wolf-skin parka, revolver in hand.

Slowly opening the door just enough to see Batiste clearly over his gun sights, Dalton said, "That's far enough, Batiste."

Batiste froze in his tracks, and then smiled as he stared at the door. Dalton realized Batiste could see part of his face looking at him through the crack of the door over the gun sights.

"*Bonjour*, Dalton Laird. Seems we meet again."

"Seems so. State your business."

Batiste smiled. "Always the one to get right down to it. Alright then. I told you once I will run you out of this valley, besides," and then Batiste's smile disappeared, "you killed my man, Hank."

"Self-defense. He fired first."

Batiste smiled again. "Well, I don't doubt that. He always was...how you say... impetuous?"

"As for the other," Dalton said, "I told *you* I would fight you for it."

"Aw, so you did. But as you can see, *monsieur*," as he gestured to the tree line, "you are outnumbered."

Hoping to plant some doubt into Batiste, Dalton said, "Maybe. Maybe not. I've been expecting you."

Batiste quickly looked around him to the hillsides surrounding the cabin, then back at Dalton. Another smile crossed his face. "I do not think so."

"Take your chances, Batiste." Then, wanting to change directions, Dalton said, "I've got witnesses you killed that Indian in Minto last winter. And, I've got a strong suspicion you killed your wife."

Batiste shrugged his shoulders. "Maybe he pull a knife on me. And my woman, maybe she slipped and fell in the Yukon."

Dalton decided to push a little more. "I heard it said you hit her over the head before she, 'slipped and fell.'"

Dalton could tell Batiste was getting upset. *Must have touched a nerve,* he thought.

"What if I did?"

Dalton heard Corrine gasp behind him, and he felt sorry for her. At least now, she had her answer.

"She had it coming to her. Always flirting with the young bucks and headstrong. What's it to ya, anyway?"

Corrine's sobbing softly and tenderly reached Dalton's brain. He fought down the urge to go to her, to hold her.

Dalton turned his attention back to Batiste and his smoldering anger erupted into flame. "Oh, didn't I tell ya? I'm a Deputy Marshal now. You're under arrest. Give yourself up, tell your men to leave, then we'll go to town and you can tell it the judge."

Dalton could see Batiste's face turn red as he raised his revolver.

"THE HELL I WILL!"

Dalton slammed the door just as two slugs plowed into the door jamb.

CHAPTER 24

Batiste wheeled, half-ran, and half-wad-dled through the snow back to the cut bank as his men fired at the cabin, covering his retreat. Sliding on his rear down the cut bank to the creek bottom, he made his way to the fire his men had kindled in an attempt to keep warm in the frigid arctic air. Flopping down next to it, he stuck out his stiffened gun hand that had been bitten by the cold blue steel. He warmed it with the meager heat the fire provided, as occasional pot shots were exchanged between his men and the cabin.

The cold, crisp air carries sound a long way and the men had heard all that was said between Batiste and Dalton.

"So, Dalton's a Deputy U.S. Marshal, now," Ward said matter-of-factly, as he squatted by the fire and poked a stick in the embers.

Batiste glanced over at him, then back to his extended hand and worked his fingers to hasten circulation of warm blood. Satisfied they were working properly, he replaced his beaver-skin mitten.

"*Oui*. At least this is what he claims. Says he's got witnesses about that Indian in Minto last winter. I don't know if he does, or no. I ain't takin' that chance. It's just all the more reason to finish him off."

"So…what do ya want to do, Boss?" Ward asked tentatively.

Batiste thought a bit. He'd underestimated Dalton. *That could prove to be fatal. He was not one to be bullied, like all the others. Besides, this Marshal business, and the possible witness, that puts a kink in things. I need time to think.*

"Keep firing at that cabin. The men can take turns warming up at the fire."

Ward left to spread the word. Batiste secreted himself behind a stump at the edge of the cut bank to watch the cabin. As his men and the cabin exchanged gunfire, it seemed at times like there were two people inside shooting back. He wasn't quite sure because of all the noise.

Upon further observation, he wasn't sure where, in the cabin, the return fire came from either. Sometimes it seemed to be coming from just above ground level. An hour's worth of gun play availed nothing.

He's well-fortified in there, he thought. *Probably has enough supplies to last a few days if need be, and we're running low. Curse this cold weather.*

"WARD!" Batiste yelled.

"YEAH, BOSS?" Ward yelled back while he worked his way to Batiste.

"Send the big Swede undercover of gunfire up there and slam against that door. Maybe he can jar it open enough to see inside. Maybe even get a bullet in Dalton."

As Ward turned to leave, Batiste added, "And tell the men to aim low."

A minute later, gunfire began in earnest. Batiste watched as the Swede plowed across the clearing through the snow and into the four-inch-thick door.

The door jarred open, and Batiste saw the Swede raise his revolver, aim..., and then slowly lower it to his side. Turning, the Swede ran toward the scrimmage line, and yelled, "THEY'RE SHOOTING LOW. YOUR DA..." but he didn't finish his sentence. The Swede stumbled and fell face forward, spraying the snow crimson red.

Did he say 'they'? I was right. There is more than one in there!

"Ward, get a few sticks of that dynamite over here and start thawing it out, a stick at a time. And be careful! It's crystallized and needs to be handled delicately. I don't want ya blowin' us up, too."

"It's going to take a half hour to thaw it out properly at this temperature," Ward cautioned.

"Just get it done."

Ward retrieved a stick of the dynamite and began the tedious, stressful job of slowly thawing it out by the fire. Then, after a few minutes, he asked, "Why not just burn him out?"

Batiste sighed. "I'm sure he's well-stocked in there and I was hoping to save as much of the supplies as I can. We're running low and we're going to need them. Besides, the men can use this cabin while they're huntin' furs. Isn't that thing warmed up enough?"

"Yeah, I think so."

"*Bon*. Toss that thing at the door. Maybe we can dislodge it and get in."

Ward shoved a fuse down the center of the stick of dynamite, worked his way to the top of the bank, lit the fuse with a firebrand, and gave it a heave.

The cold, dense air amplified the concussion and set the dogs to howling and tugging on their stakeout chains. The men covered their ringing ears.

As the snow settled, Batiste could see it fell a good five feet short and was completely ineffective.

"*Sacre.*' Thaw out another one, you passel o' cowards, and get it to the door this time! Ward, you throw like *petite fille*. Get Gee pole Larson over here. Maybe he can do better."

Another half hour was spent thawing out a second stick. Batiste watched as Gee pole, with shaking hands, shoved a fuse down the dynamite stick's center.

Grabbing the end of a flaming brand from the fire, he worked his way to the top of the cut bank, established a sure footing, blew on the smoldering firebrand, and touched it to the fuse. Instantly, it sputtered to life. He rose to heave it across the clearing to the cabin door.

A bullet ripped through his chest. He crumpled in a heap and rolled down the embankment. The stick of dynamite landed by his head. As everyone dove for cover and covered their ears, Ward grabbed it, climbed the bank, and heaved it as hard as he could. The dynamite thumped against the door.

Once again, the dogs howled in protest at the explosion. And, once again, the dynamite had no effect on the well-built cabin.

Batiste could not believe it. "How much dynamite do we have left?"

"About three pounds," Ward answered.

"Bundle it all together. I'll get him out of there, one way or another!"

"What about the cabin? You'll destroy it."

"*Sacre*,' Ward. At this point, I don't care. Just do it!"

It took another thirty minutes to thaw out the rest of the dynamite. The men kept up a steady barrage against the cabin.

Ward recruited another man to carry the bundle to its destination. Coming in from the north side, away from the window, he successfully tossed it onto the roof.

At detonation, Batiste was instantly confident that it had done its job. He satisfactorily watched chunks of timber and splintered wood sail through the air.

With pieces of wood raining down, Batiste ordered his men to storm what was left of Dalton's cabin. Rushing forward, he saw no movement at first and hoped his adversary was dead.

Upon reaching the front of the cabin, he realized there was a pit in the floor, half-filled with debris. It moved. Batiste's men raised their rifles. But Batiste was fascinated to see if Dalton had survived. He gave the order not to fire.

Still watching in fascination, Batiste's heart skipped a beat as he watched a figure rising like a Sphinx from the rubble.

Standing in front of him, dazed and bleeding, was Corrine.

CHAPTER 25

Dalton became aware of a heavy, stifling, almost suffocating weight of splintered timbers and moss from part of the collapsed roof, pressing down on him as he slowly regained consciousness.

His ears rang, but he could hear the voice of the man he hated, and remembered the tremendous explosion overhead, as he, Corrine, and Bandit huddled together in the root cellar.

Where's Corrine? Is she alright? The thought clamped on his brain with the suddenness of a steel trap.

Looking around through the floating fog of dust, his eyes fell on the lifeless form of his beloved lead dog, Bandit. A splintered piece of the ridgepole had pierced her chest. Looking further, he saw no sign of Corrine. Mustering all of his strength, his arms exploded upward and scattered the debris off himself and Bandit.

Gathering her up in his arms, he stood and fixed his eyes on the astonished faces of the men surrounding him. Rage and wretchedness boiled up from deep inside, and manifested itself with an anguished roar. The men scattered as Dalton climbed out of the root cellar with the lifeless body of Bandit.

Dalton gently carried Bandit's limp body towards the cache, knelt down, and lovingly laid her on a patch of undisturbed, brilliant white snow, gleaming with a million diamond points of reflected light.

Unconcerned with the distant echo of the riot of desperate men, bullets whizzing by and shouts of anger, Dalton stroked Bandit's head and neck, drug his shirt sleeve across his dimmed eyes and said his last good-bye.

Suddenly, a hand was on his shoulder. Dalton spun to his feet with the agility of a lynx, fist cocked back, ready to strike, and breathing heavy from the adrenaline-induced panic.

"Easy, easy pardner," the man said, with both hands raised and backing up a step.

Dalton relaxed and lowered his arm as he gazed at the bearded face of Yukon Jack. His eyes searching Jack's, he said, "Anything I've ever loved either leaves me or dies." Recognizing fully that it was indeed, Yukon Jack, he asked, "When did you get here?"

"A couple minutes ago. Me, Ollie, and Dreibelbis was coming down that ridge when we heard a 'BOOM' and saw your cabin disintegrate."

Dalton looked around while Jack spoke.

"Figured you and Corrine were holed up in there."

Seeing Deputy Marshal Dreibelbis putting cuffs on one of the men, Dalton tossed his head in recognition as their eyes met. The weapons had been stacked in a pile in the clearing in front of what was left of the cabin.

"Had you two figured for dead, too. But as we came into the clearing, you climbed up outta that hole with Bandit in your arms and gave a blood-curdling, lonesome wail. I sez to myself, they ain't no way anybody can kill that man."

Not seeing what he was looking for, Dalton asked, "Where's Corrine?" as he pushed past Jack and headed to the pile of rubble.

Jack turned to face Dalton. "Wait. She's not there."

Dalton stopped, and turned back to Jack. "Where *is* she?"

"About the time you were climbing up outta that hole, Batiste was draggin' Corrine a- kickin' and a-fightin' down to the creek bottom. I saw him give her a cuff upside the head. Me, Dreibelbis, and Ollie had our hands full with these guys. Then, I caught a glimpse of Batiste driving a team down the trail towards the North Fork. Looked like he was usin' his dog-whip on Corrine trying to keep her in the sled."

"Jack, I need a parka. I'm freezing my tail off. Find one and some mittens and meet me in the creek bottom. I'm going after her and I'm going to bring Batiste in for murder." Then, on second thought, Dalton added, "And, find my rifle too!"

In the creek bottom, Dalton quickly scanned the dog teams staked out by Batiste's men. With subconscious judgment, he picked a team that looked the healthiest, with bright eyes, good conformation, and an eagerness to pull. Choosing one of their teams gave him the advantage of saving time because they were already harnessed. All he had to do was clip them into the tug lines. Besides, his team was without a leader now, and he knew that would cause problems as each dog fought for the coveted position.

Choosing a sturdy, lightweight birch sled, he emptied the basket of its contents and hooked up the team, as the other dogs howled their dismay and jumped up and down wanting to go, too. His hands were so cold, he had to stop after hooking up each dog and warm his stiffened hands and fingers under his armpits. His ears tingled and burned from frostbite, just as Jack returned with his parka, mittens, martin-skin hat, and rifle.

Dawning his parka and fur hat, Dalton shoved the 30-30 in the scabbard, then blew warm air into his stiffened, cupped hands and rubbed them together to hasten blood flow.

"I found this in the rubble. It's Corrine's parka. She's going to get mighty cold." Jack said as he lashed it and a rabbit skin blanket in the sled basket. "You think you can catch up to them?"

Dalton mentally calculated time and distance as he pulled on his mittens and worked his fingers. "Batiste is carrying a load. I'm not. Barring any trouble, I should catch them before we make the mouth of the North Fork."

No sooner had Jack finished lashing the parka and blanket down, Dalton pulled the snow hook and yelled, "HIKE!"

Five eager huskies and a lightweight birch sled with Dalton riding the runners flew down the creek bottom toward the left-hand turn onto the hillside trail. Pushing his right foot on the outside runner and leaning to the inside curve, the flexible little sled tracked the curve beautifully.

Now on his well-brushed trail, the dogs settled into their ground-eating lope. Holding onto the handlebar, Dalton stepped off the runners and jogged behind a few yards to create some warmth, being mindful not to overdo it and start breathing through his mouth. At twenty-seven below, one could frostbite their throat and lungs.

Within a couple of miles, Dalton found sign there had been trouble. Breaking his sled to a stop, he read the story written in the disturbed snow by the trail.

Batiste's sled had overturned. Drag marks showed plainly where the driver had held on and frantically fought the dogs to a halt. A body-sized hole in the fresh snow beside the trail where the drag mark started, told Dalton Corrine had bailed out of the sled.

She was injured, for spots of blood were the evidence. He didn't know if she was injured in the blast or from Batiste's beatings.

Probably a little of both, Dalton decided. Batiste's footprints in the trail told Dalton he had gone back and forced her back into the sled.

Amazed, Dalton thought, *She's a fighter. She bought me some time. Poor girl must be freezing.*

A couple more miles down the trail, Dalton saw Corrine lying in the snow by the trail.

Dalton stood on the brake and yelled, "WHOA!"

The dogs jerked to a stop and he stomped the snow hook into the trail. Not taking any chances of the dogs pulling free and running off, he quickly tied the sled to a nearby tree.

Dalton carried Corrine to the sled. Corrine tried to speak but he could see that she was too cold to form words. Her cheeks, nose, and fingertips were chalk white, indicating ice crystals in the blood, and there was a laceration across one cheekbone with frozen blood.

Dalton helped her put on her parka and wrapped her legs in the blanket, then gently placed her in the sled basket. Taking off his mittens, he placed his now warm hands on her face to help thaw her cheeks and nose. Then, he took her cold hands in his.

"I need to arrest your father." Dalton saw a flash of hate in her eyes as she carefully formed the words through her stiffened blue lips.

"He's...n...no father...of...ma, mine!"

Dalton's jaw muscles tightened. *He's going to pay for this.*

Standing back up, he took a pinch of Copenhagen, put the can away, replaced his mittens.

"Stay bundled up in that blanket and cover your head. Keep as much warmth trapped inside as possible. And hang on."

CHAPTER 26

Dalton coaxed the unfamiliar dogs as best he could, and tried to make up distance and time. Batiste now had the advantage with an empty sled. Soon, Dalton caught a glimpse through the trees of Batiste as he descended off the hillside trail down onto the flats, heading for the mouth of the North Fork.

If he gets to the main cabin, it'll be the same thing all over again. Only it'll be me *trying to roust* him *out,* he thought. *I gotta do something.* Thinking of nothing else, and out of desperation, he hollered at the dogs, "MUSH YOU HUSKIES. MUSH FOR ALL YOU'RE WORTH!"

Instantly, they leaped into a fast gallop and Dalton almost catapulted over backward. Only the quick grab of the handlebar saved him.

Well, that did it. They must be used to being yelled at.

As Dalton and Corrine came down onto the flats, he could see Batiste, only a mile ahead, cross the Salcha and disappear over the bank and into the brush on the other side.

Soon, Dalton's team crossed the river and climbed the same bank. Remembering that after climbing the bank, the trail made a right-hand turn onto the main trail, Dalton slowed the dogs a bit to avoid whipping the sled into the brush on the opposite side. Sort of like the childhood game of crack-the-whip.

Dalton wondered if Batiste had successfully negotiated that turn, and then made a bet with himself that he hadn't.

The bet was settled when the sled made the turn and a pistol shot ricocheted through the tree limbs next to Dalton's head. Corrine uncovered her head and looked back at Dalton.

"Cover up and stay down!" Dalton hissed.

Ducking down behind the handlebar, Dalton stood on the break and retrieved the snow-hook from the boot hanging from the crosspiece just under the handlebar. When the sled finally came to a stop, Dalton was able to wrap the hook with its rope around a convenient alder.

"Stay in the sled and don't move," he told Corrine in a hushed voice.

Looking around, Dalton saw that Batiste had spilled his sled negotiating the turn and that the dogs had gotten away from him. Batiste was afoot, somewhere ahead.

Slowly, Dalton reached up, and slid the Winchester out of the scabbard. He eased the lever down just enough to make sure there was a round chambered, then closed the action and cocked the hammer.

"Stay here," he whispered to Corrine. "I'm going after him."

Fixing his eyes on the brush and trees ahead, he crouched and moved from behind the sled, slipped and fell against a nearby tree. Snow, dislodged from the impact, cascaded down over him and the rifle. Some of it fell down his back.

Seeing no movement ahead, he shook the snow from the hood of his parka and dug the snow out from around his neck.

You fool! Watch where you place your feet! he scolded himself.

Dalton worked his way up the trail from tree to tree, following Batiste's footprints in the snow.

Dalton caught a glimpse of movement through the trees. Straining his eyes in the lowering light, Dalton recognized Batiste's wolf-skin parka as it blended in and disappeared into willow brush lining a sand bar. Batiste was making his way to the river.

That's odd, Dalton mused. *Why not stay on the packed trail and pick a spot to ambush me? Why is he wading through deep snow, leaving a trail a blind man could follow?*

Dalton followed Batiste's tracks back up the trail and found where Batiste had left it.

Looking around, he found another set of prints. A large wolf had entered the trail ahead of Batiste.

Evidently, caught between the wolf in front and Dalton behind, Batiste had bailed off the trail and headed for the river.

The wolf's prints followed Batiste through the willows by the tracks he'd left behind.

Hearing a noise behind him, Dalton turned and found Corrine standing there, still wrapped in the white snowshoe-hare blanket.

"Be careful what you do," she said.

Dalton smiled. "I'm always careful. Are you alright?"

"I'm okay. I'm warm enough."

"Good. Stay here, I'm going in after him."

"No. I go with you," she said, matter-of-factly.

If there's one thing I've learned, it's that when she makes up her mind, there's no changing it, he thought.

"Okay, but stay close. If shootin' starts, get down."

Dalton turned and stepped into Batiste's tracks, as the wolf had, and followed them as quickly as he dared. Thirty yards into the thicket, Dalton saw the wolf had jumped the trail and had taken off to the left.

Wonder where the wolf's going? Then, the thought crossed his mind that he'd not seen the last of the wolf.

Continuing on, they followed Batiste's tracks and soon came out onto the gravel bar, devoid of brush, on the inside curve of a bend in the river.

Up ahead, on the river ice, stood Batiste. He faced Dalton and Corrine, with his back against the high, outside bank of the river. On his right, and on his left, were Sweepers—toppled birch and spruce trees, still connected to the bank that had fallen into the river during the summer, and frozen in the ice. Batiste was trapped with no place to turn.

"How in the world did he get himself into a corner like that?" Dalton asked half aloud.

Just then, Batiste raised his revolver and fired three rounds at something in the brush to Dalton's left. Dalton ducked and looked to see what Batiste fired at. Then, shouldering the rifle, Dalton hollered, "BATISTE, YOU'RE STILL UNDER ARREST! DROP YOUR WEA—" He didn't have time to finish.

Batiste swung on Dalton and Corrine and fired two more rounds.

"Get down!" Dalton commanded.

Mentally counting the shots, Dalton decided Batiste's gun had to be empty.

Standing back up, he ordered, "DROP THAT WEAPON!"

Batiste again swung to his right and pulled the trigger. The hammer fell on an empty shell casing with an unmistakable 'CLICK'.

"*ZHOH ZHRAII!*" Corrine exclaimed.

Dalton looked at her, and then downstream in the direction she was looking.

Dalton saw the black wolf, crouched low, working his way directly to Batiste. Dalton realized why the wolf's tracks left Batiste's trail. The wolf had outflanked Batiste and driven him onto the river ice.

Dalton heard the river ice pop. "DON'T MOVE!" he yelled.

Looking back at the wolf, Dalton could see that it had closed the distance by half.

Batiste's movement caught Dalton's eye, and he watched as Batiste took another step backward and again pulled the trigger on the revolver. And, once again, the hammer fell on an empty shell casing. Batiste threw his useless revolver at the wolf as the river ice popped and cracked.

Dalton raised his rifle and aimed at the wolf. He hesitated, not wanting to kill the black wolf—apparently, the only survivor of the pack. All of the others lost to the poison baits left out by the order of that man on the ice.

He deserves whatever that wolf gives him. Dalton lowered his rifle. Then, on second thought, *No, that wouldn't be right.* Dalton raised the rifle and steadied his aim.

"No!" Corrine grabbed his arm. "This was meant to be."

Dalton shrugged her off and steadied the rifle. "A man's life's at stake. Even though he doesn't deserve it."

Again, the ominous popping of the river ice filled the cold subarctic air. Dalton's finger tightened on the trigger. He felt the trigger sear disengage, but the expected recoil never materialized. Lowering his rifle, Dalton looked at it, puzzled. *What happened?* he wondered. Then he saw it.

Dalton had neglected to check his weapon after the snow fell on him. Snow had packed itself between the hammer and the firing pin, rendering it useless for anything but a club. Frantically, Dalton kicked through the snow trying to find a twig, anything, to dig out the packed snow.

Out of his peripheral vision, Dalton saw Corrine rush forward, toward the wolf. Dalton made a grab for her but missed.

He watched Corrine stop a couple of yards from the wolf. Dalton moved up beside her to protect her as the wolf turned his head and looked at them both. Dalton had seen that same look in Bandit's eyes—the daughter of this black wolf—and knew he and Corrine were in no danger.

The wolf turned its attention back to Jon Batiste on the ice. It curled its upper lip and bared its fangs. A low, throaty growl rumbled from deep inside its chest. With the quickness and agility born of a predator, the wolf rushed Batiste.

Batiste hollered in panic and took a step backward. The ice cracked loudly, then a thousand little crackling sounds continued.

Dalton and Corrine watched Batiste disappear through the ice, with nothing but the wolf-skin parka momentarily floating on the surface. Then, it, too, slowly disappeared, pulled under by the current.

The wolf turned and faced Corrine and Dalton. It 'huffed' once, then twice, trotted past them on the river ice, and vanished into the willow brush.

CHAPTER 27

D alton walked into the Federal Marshal's Office and sat down at Dreibelbis' desk.

"That was a strange report you wrote." Dreibelbis pointed to a stack of papers on his desk.

Dalton rested his elbows on the chair arms, pressed the fingers of both hands together in front of his belly, and sighed deeply, thinking over the events of Batiste's death six days ago.

After Batiste went through the ice, Dalton got Corrine to the main cabin. Ollie had thoughtfully sent his woman after Dalton and Corrine to help any way she could while he, Yukon Jack, and Dreibelbis marched the rest of the gang back to Fairbanks down the Chena winter trail.

Dalton and Ollie's woman took care of Corrine the best they could. She had suffered frostbite to her fingertips and nose, which were blistered and tender to the touch. Luckily, she would not lose anything. They also bandaged up her lacerated cheek and a few other cuts and bruises they found.

The next morning, Ollie's woman took Corrine to Fairbanks via the Valdez trail. Dalton mushed back to the upper cabin on Gold Creek and spent five hours thawing and digging a spot of frozen ground to provide a proper resting place for Bandit.

Turning his own dogs loose, he mushed back to the main cabin, picking up as many poisoned wolves and foxes and wolverines as he could find, hoping against hope that none of his dogs would find the tainted bait. He ended up losing two more dogs.

During all this time, Dalton couldn't get the circumstances of the black wolf and Batiste out of his mind. It played repeatedly through his brain like a song you can't shake, as it was doing, now.

"I can understand you're questioning it, and when I think on it, I don't understand exactly why things happened as they did. But I can assure you, everything I wrote in my report is true."

Dreibelbis smiled, looked down at the report on his desk then back up.

"Dalton, I'm not questioning your truthfulness. I know you too well. It just seems strange. The coincidences, that is."

"I've asked myself the question over and over, was it coincidence the wolf was there, or... was it something else? Corrine, of course, doesn't believe it was mere coincidence. Like the northern lights, I guess there're some things we may never understand."

They both sat silently. Dalton lost in his thoughts and Dreibelbis apparently so.

Then Dalton asked, "What about the rest of the gang?"

Dreibelbis leaned back in his chair. "Most of 'em were hired a month ago to work for Batiste. The only thing we really have to hold 'em on is resisting arrest. Yukon Jack blames Batiste and Ward for leaving him for dead, not any of the other men. Speaking of Ward, seems the Canadian Mounties have been looking for him. We got a wire requesting we hold him until spring breakup, then they'll come down the Yukon on the first riverboat and take custody. He has a prison sentence to serve."

Dalton nodded his head. "Good. That takes care of that."

Dalton rubbed his hands on his pant legs and was about ready to get up and leave when Dreibelbis asked with a smile, "You goin' to the Halloween Masquerade roller-skatin' party at Gordon's Roller Rink this evening?"

Dalton laughed as he stood up, "No, that's no place for me. I just got in from the Salcha this morning. Sold the furs, paid hospital bills, and wrote that report. I'm tired. Besides, I'm afraid I'd break my neck, as well as my dignity."

Dreibelbis' smile disappeared. With a serious voice, he said, "You need to go. Corrine said she would be there."

Dalton's smile disappeared too, as he realized something was up. "Oh, I don't know...I've had trouble before..."

"Yeah, yeah," Dreibelbis interrupted. "I've heard all that before. You know she's the best thing that's happened to you. But you're stubborn. You'll let her walk out of your life, then one day you'll look up and see the end is near and wonder what it would have been like with her by your side. And you'll die a bitter, old man, all alone in one of your line cabins. And maybe in a year, or maybe two, someone will find your bones picked clean by the lemmings and voles. But hey..." Dreibelbis threw up his hands. "Who am I to tell another man how to live? Go back out in the bush an' wallow in self-pity. You don't need a woman in your life."

Dalton's jaw muscles tightened. "Don't tell me what I need or don't need. Who says I don't need a woman?"

"Why, you've said as much yourself."

"Well, that was before..."

"Before what?"

"Never mind. I'm going back to the Nordale to get ready." Dalton headed for the door.

"Get ready? For what?"

Dalton opened the door, looked back at Dreibelbis who had a smirk on his face.

"To go roller-skatin'. What else? And don't look at me like that. It's called progress."

* * *

Dalton Laird walked through the door of Gordon's Roller Rink and stepped to the side. Couples and singles dressed in costume, some wearing masks, whirled and glided under bright electric lights in a large circle on the hardwood floor. In the balcony and along the walls, people moved about while watching the skaters. Along one wall, refreshments were available—everything from soda to suds.

Dalton ascended the staircase to the balcony to get a better view of the crowd below. Soon, he spied Yukon Jack, decked out in a smoke-tanned moose-hide jacket, decorated with beads and quill work. With his beard and long hair, he briefly reminded Dalton of Buffalo Bill.

Dalton scanned the area Jack had come from, looking for one thing...Corrine. And he found her.

Her long chestnut hair, a stark contrast to the other women's hairstyles, was tied in a ponytail and spilled down the back of her pink, full-length gown.

Dalton watched her for a minute, then thought, *No. No, she's too good for the likes of me. She'd never be interested.*

As Dalton watched her, she turned her head and locked eyes with him. She smiled then, and so help him, he grinned.

Dalton turned and made his way through the crowd, down the staircase, and across the floor to her. As they met, Dalton kissed her and she did not resist. He continued kissing her until he heard someone close by loudly clearing his or her throat. Breaking the embrace, Dalton turned.

"Hey now, big fella. This is a family affair," Yukon Jack stood there with two glasses of lemonade.

"Hum? Oh yeah," Dalton scanned the crowd, and then blushed as he realized people were watching. Some of the ladies had a look of consternation on their face, while others smiled.

"Pardon us, ladies," Dalton said. Then, turning to Corrine, "Let's find a place to sit."

Finding an empty table, Dalton politely seated Corrine then took his seat. Yukon Jack offered her and Dalton the lemonade.

"No, no that's yours. I'll get some later," said Dalton.

"That's okay. I prefer something else, anyway. Besides, you two have things to talk about," Jack said, as he turned to leave.

Dalton faced Corrine, "When you looked directly at me on the balcony, it seemed as if you knew I'd be there."

Corrine smiled. "Intuition. By the way, I've missed you the last few days."

Dalton looked down at his hands. "Yeah, I've had some fixin' up and cleanin' up to do. Not to mention writin' reports." Then, looking up at her, said, "I always hated that part."

"Well, you're here now. I'm sorry about Bandit. I know she meant the world to you."

Dalton looked at the table, and sighed deeply. "Yes, she did. But I'll always have the memories."

Wanting to change the subject, he looked back into her eyes.

"I guess the Amanita is yours now. Givin' any thought as to what you might do with it?"

Corrine took a sip of the lemonade and set the glass down on the table.

"Yesterday, Jack introduced me to a man who offered me a teaching position to the Indian kids in Salchaket. I'm thinking about taking it and selling the Amanita to pay off Father's debts."

Dalton smiled.

"What?" she asked.

"I'm just thinking how well everything turned out."

"For instance?"

"Well, for instance, meeting you. Your job will be close to home while I run the trapline. Hey, you can even teach our kids. We'll have a good life together."

"Aren't you forgetting something?" she asked with a slight smile.

Dalton thought a bit, then said, "Well... no. Not that I know of."

"If we have kids, don't you think the proper thing to do is get married?"

"Oh... yeah... Will you marry me, Corrine?" Dalton asked, as he blushed.

Corrine smiled. "Of course!"

R ussell M. Chace is the author of the Alaska historical fiction novel *From Out of The Loneliness*. As a teenager and young adult, he learned much of what he writes, along the traplines and rivers he traveled by snowshoe, dog team and snow machine. It was during those years he wrote multiple articles for Alaska Magazine, Fishing and Hunting News, Voice of the Trapper and the Alaska trapper.

After moving to Colorado with his wife and two boys, Russell earned a degree in Criminal Justice and worked for the Colorado Department of Corrections for over twenty-two years. During that time, he was a member of the Emergency Response Team and the Escape Team, tracking escaped inmates in urban and suburban environments.

Russell is now retired and currently hard at work on his newest Alaska historical fiction novel. When not writing, he can be found fly-fishing, hunting, or prospecting the Arkansas River in the Rocky Mountains.

Made in the USA
Monee, IL
13 September 2021

77979398R00140